The Next GREAT JANE

K. L. GOING

Dial Books for Young Readers

Dial Books for Young Readers
An imprint of Penguin Random House LLC, New York

First published in the United States of America by Dial Books for Young Readers, 2020
First paperback edition published 2021

Visit us online at penguinrandomhouse.com.

THE LIBRARY OF CONGRESS HAS CATALOGED THE HARDCOVER EDITION AS FOLLOWS:
Names: Going, K. L. (Kelly L.) author. Title: The next great Jane / K. L. Going.
Description: New York : Dial Books for Young Readers, [2020] | Audience: Ages 10–14. | Audience: Grades 7–9. | Summary: "Jane, a budding writer and Jane Austen fan, discovers the true secret to writing when a famous author and her cute, but annoying, son come to her small coastal town and play seemingly unwitting roles in affecting the custody battle between Jane's Hollywood mother and marine biologist father"— Provided by publisher. Identifiers: LCCN 2019038768 (print) | LCCN 2019038769 (ebook) |
ISBN 9780803734753 (hardcover) | ISBN 9780698408777 (ebook)
Subjects: CYAC: Authors—Fiction. | Custody of children—Fiction. | Remarriage—Fiction. | Friendship—Fiction. | Family life—Fiction. | Maine—Fiction.
Classification: LCC PZ7.G559118 Nex 2020 (print) | LCC PZ7.G559118 (ebook) | DDC

Printed in the United States of America

ISBN 9780147517760

10 9 8 7 6 5 4 3 2 1

Design by Cerise Steel
Text set in Calisto MT

.

For Ashton Paul Adams

CHAPTER ONE

*N*othing important ever happened in Whickett Harbor, Maine. So, it figured that the two biggest things to hit the town in a decade would occur on the exact same night. One of them even threatened to cancel out the other, but I was not about to let a hurricane keep me from meeting a best-selling author.

Little did I know, the hurricane would bring more trouble than I bargained for, including: the most annoying boy I'd ever met, a night of disaster, and worst of all . . . my mother, fresh from Hollywood.

Well, you know what they say: a good story is full of trouble.

"Emmett? Jane? Anyone home?" The voice drifting through the front door belonged to the coolest person I knew. Ana

Taylor was my babysitter, our housekeeper, car fixer-upper, weekly planner, and all around Most Important Person Ever. Without Ana, Dad and I would be lost.

"In here!" me and Dad called out at the exact same time.

For Dad, "in here" meant he had his head stuck in the refrigerator, making sure he wasn't missing any stray jars of seawater. He's an ocean scientist, and there's only one way to describe how he feels about his plankton samples: *true love*.

For me, "in here" meant I was in my writing nook. Our old-fashioned kitchen has a huge cupboard set into the wall that used to have shelves until Ana knocked the top ones out with a sledge hammer. As long as I bring a flashlight, it's the best place to create, like I'm in a hobbit hole or a secret compartment.

Ana sighed. "Should've known. Either of you planning on emerging any time soon?"

I swung open the cupboard door and jumped down. "Please, *please* tell me that the library event hasn't been canceled."

"Hello to you too, Jane." Ana tousled my hair. She's known me since I was in kindergarten, so she's allowed. "It's still on. They really don't want to call it off."

In the whole history of the town, there had never been

an event of this magnitude, and if we canceled now, J. E. Fairfax might never come back.

Ana frowned. "Emmett?"

Dad tried to emerge from the refrigerator, bumped his head, then smacked his hand when he went to touch the bumped spot. Dad is tall, built like a lumberjack with broad shoulders, and he frequently collides with the furniture in our old house. "Ooh. Oh. Ouch. Sorry. Hello, Ana."

He scrunched up his nose and chuckled as if he knew exactly how nerdy he was.

"You're staying home tonight, right?" Ana pressed. "Weather report says the brunt of the storm won't hit until ten, but the wind's picking up already."

Dad shook his head. "Got to get these samples to the lab in case our power goes out. I'll probably sleep there. Need to make sure nothing gets damaged."

Dad regularly gathered samples on his boat and then carted them home until he could return to the lab. It was a standing rule that no one ever ate or drank anything from our fridge that wasn't clearly labeled.

"Really?" Ana frowned. "Shouldn't you stay here with Jane?"

My father scratched his chin as if that idea hadn't occurred to him. "Right. Yes. Maybe I should come back.

It's just . . ." He gave Ana the pleading face he reserved for convincing her to work extra hours. "These samples are invaluable resources for the oceanography community around the globe. If anything happened at the lab, we'd have *lost them*."

He seemed to think we should be horrified at the idea.

Ana put her hands on both hips. "Oh no, Emmett Brannen. Those big brown eyes of yours aren't going to sway me this time. The fact is, you wouldn't have to worry about these samples if you'd learned to work the generator like I told you."

Dad looked shame-faced. The thing about generators is that they aren't as simple as most people think. You don't just throw a switch when your power goes out. You've got to maintain a generator—turn it on periodically and make sure all of the spark plugs and such are working. I'd heard Ana remind Dad about it a hundred times, but no matter what, when it came time to flick that switch, our generator was never in working condition.

Ana was a petite blond spitfire. She could chop a cord of wood, outwork half the men in the Whickett Harbor Volunteer Fire Department, and fix your flatbed truck in her spare time. The only thing Dad could do with your flatbed truck was remember where he parked it.

If you were lucky.

"Ana," he said, "these are red tide samples from off Monhegan Island."

She just narrowed her eyes.

Dad shuffled his feet. "Well . . . Jane could come with me and we could sleep at the lab."

"No. Way." I shook my head. "I am *not* missing J. E. Fairfax's talk. You know I've been waiting for this forever."

Dad raised one eyebrow in my direction. "Forever, huh? You're only twelve. Besides, she doesn't even write for kids; she writes trashy romance novels. I'm pretty sure all of her advice will be aimed at adults."

"Her novels are *not* trashy, Dad," I argued. "The *New York Times* called them 'sweeping, romantic sagas full of high drama.'" The library had used that quote on their posters, and I'd memorized it because it sounded incredible. "Every one of her books is a best seller, and three of them have been made into movies."

Ana grinned dreamily. "I *adore* her movies. There are always two people who are meant for each other, but they can't see the truth until fate forces them together."

"Remember that one with the guy in the military who moved away from his childhood sweetheart? Then years later they found each other again—"

"Oh, I loved that one!" Ana clapped excitedly.

Dad cleared his throat, giving us his best bewildered expression. "Could we get back to the point? Ana, could you, possibly—"

"Uh-uh." Ana crossed her arms over her chest. "I need to be at my apartment to look in on Mrs. Wallace next door. She practically had a conniption when I left to get Jane. She's so worked up about this storm, she'll probably have a stroke."

"We could do rock, paper, scissors," Dad suggested.

Ana threw her hands up. "No! We couldn't. You need to stay home with your daughter. Period!"

There was a long moment of silence where none of us said a word, but finally my father relented. "Okay. You're right. I'll pick Jane up at the library after these samples are stored properly, and I'll ask Marty to check in on the lab later tonight."

Ana beamed. "Thank you. I knew you'd make the right choice." She practically glowed.

Dad ran a hand through his sandy blond hair, making it stick out in weird directions. "Well, I'd better get moving if I'm going to be back in time. Thanks for dropping Jane off at the author thing." He picked up one of the coolers, then paused. "You know you're amazing, right?"

Dad had been telling Ana that for years. She blushed and made the same scoffing noise she usually made.

As Dad walked past, he nudged me in the ribs. "Have fun. Remember this night when you're supporting me in my old age with the fortune you make on your writing."

I rolled my eyes. "Your jokes are terrible."

Dad grinned and I shoved him the rest of the way out the door. He loaded the coolers in the back of the truck, then climbed into the cab and leaned out the open window. "Once we get home, we can watch movies until the lights go out. We've got popcorn and dill seasoning, right sprite?"

Those were the only two grocery items Dad never forgot to stock up on.

"Yup." I waved as he backed out.

Sounded perfect. A chance to learn the tricks of the writing trade from a famous author, followed by a whole evening hanging out with my father during a hurricane? What more could a girl ask for?

Too bad that's not even close to how the evening turned out.

CHAPTER TWO

My best friend, Kitty, wants to be a model, and she's willing to suffer for it. I've watched her freeze in an off-the-shoulder sweater mid-winter, squeeze her feet into pointy-toed heels, chase after flimsy hand-knitted berets when the sea breeze snatched them off her head, and wriggle her bottom into pants two sizes too small.

Writers, on the other hand, are allowed to look any way we want, but tonight was a special occasion. The only authors the library had ever hosted were Twyla Jenkins, who'd written *The Downeast Guide to Lobster Casseroles,* and Georgie Doyle, who'd written a memoir called *The One that Got Away.* So, when news came around that the internationally known romance author J. E. Fairfax would be in town, they'd planned a cocktail party—the height of sophistication. I didn't want anyone to say I wasn't just as committed to my future as Kitty, so I'd done something I hadn't done for ten years.

I'd put on a dress.

I knew it had been ten years, because the last time I'd worn a dress was right before my mother moved to California. She'd gotten me all dolled up for a mother-daughter photo. We had matching pink gowns and sparkly tiaras. I'm only two years old, but I have on lip gloss, blush, and real diamond earrings. My not-quite curly hair is twirled into jet-black ringlets, and Mom's hair is styled to match. We look utterly ridiculous.

To top it all off, Mom hadn't thought things out very well, because the ear piercings were brand-new. She'd taken me to Claire's boutique right before we got our pictures taken and I'd screamed my head off, so my face is all red and blotchy beneath the makeup.

When Dad tells this story it sounds like the funniest thing ever, but we both know that the very next day Mom moved to California to become an actress. Now she's got the framed 8 x 10 version of that photo hanging on the wall of her apartment, and when I make my mandatory visits, she points it out and says, "Sweet baby Jane. We've always been so close."

In what universe?

Some of the kids at school find it hard to believe that I've never been close with my mother, but when you haven't lived with someone for a decade, and you only see them twice a year, it's hard to feel like you really know them. I guess I think of my mom more like an aunt—a distant aunt who is my polar opposite.

If Mom were making me get dressed up tonight, I'd have dug in my heels, but since J. E. Fairfax was about to offer me the keys to my future, I wanted to look grown-up and sophisticated when I met her. Who knows? Maybe someday she'd remember the time she met Jane Brannen, future award-winning author, in Whickett Harbor, Maine.

As I checked my dress in the mirror for the hundredth time, Ana tapped her foot. "Can you move a little faster, Jane? You don't want to be late."

"Are you sure this isn't too baggy?" I asked. I'd had to borrow a dress from Kitty, and like most of her wardrobe, it was pink, black, and white—the signature colors of the Hello Kitty brand. The bottom half had a silky fabric and the top half was plain pink with a cat face on the pocket. Kitty insisted the cat face was retro-chic.

"The dress looks great," Ana said, tapping her fingers on our kitchen island. "It's adorable. Very retro. Kitty knows what she's doing."

I grinned.

You wouldn't think we'd be best friends, but Kitty is like my sister. Her parents died when she was small, so her grandmother (everyone calls her Granny V) raised her.

Dad practically adopted her as well. When I got a tree fort, he built one for Kitty too. When I got a tire swing, so did Kitty. If there was a father-daughter event, he took us both. Granny V called herself my honorary grandmother because it was understood that Kitty and I were a pair.

Even though Kitty didn't like to write, she did love to draw, so all our lives we'd created stories as a team. Our longest one was *Two Princesses of Penmore,* where Kitty found out that she was the undiscovered heiress to the Hello Kitty fortune. She inherited the Penmore Estate and we moved in together.

The Penmore Estate was a real place—a beautiful old mansion about a half hour from Whickett Harbor. It was tucked away in the woods, surrounded by a wrought iron fence, and no one I knew had ever been inside. Kitty and I were sure it was full of chandeliers, marble statues, spiral staircases, and ghosts of wealthy people.

While Kitty was busy pretending to be an heiress, I liked to pretend that I was descended from Jane Austen, one of the most famous writers of all time. She's also Ana's favorite author. Even when I was small, we'd curl up together and watch the movie versions of her books. Since Jane Austen lived in England during the 1800s, all of her stories take place in that time period. There are floofy dresses, men in strange-looking pants, and lots of fancy language, but I don't mind. Ana loves the romance of it all, and I love Ana, so things that make her happy make me happy too.

Now though, Ana frowned, staring out the window. "It sure is getting dark out there."

I knew I'd better hurry up before she changed her mind about letting me go. "I'm ready."

Ana looked me over with a critical eye. "Something is missing."

"Really?" I looked down at my dress. It wasn't exactly sophisticated, but I *did* have dangly earrings and matching shoes.

"You need a necklace." Ana pulled a small box from her jacket pocket and handed it to me.

I wanted to throw my arms around her, but first I opened the box to see what was inside. Usually, I didn't wear jewelry, but the necklace was perfect. The chain was a burnished bronze, and at the end was a small metal book charm. When I opened it, there was a dark silhouette of a woman's profile on one side, and on the other side in flowing script, it said: *Indulge your imagination in every possible flight. Jane Austen.*

"I almost got you the one that said 'obstinate, headstrong girl,'" Ana said, laughing, "but I chose this one instead. They're handmade." She paused. "I think every writer needs a talisman. Something to bring them luck. Don't you agree?"

I nodded, unable to speak while my nose was sniffling and my eyes welled up. Ana pulled me into a hug and kissed the top of my head.

"You're going to be the next great Jane," she told me. "I've always said so." For just a moment her voice was soft and wistful, but then she gave me a playful shove. "Except if we're late, because then you'll be a dismal failure."

I laughed, then wiped my eyes and followed her out to her truck. "Thanks," I said, fingering the necklace. "I love it."

Ana grinned. "Had to do something to mark this occasion."

I shook my head, pondering the magnitude of what was about to happen. "Who would've thought a famous author would ever come to Whickett Harbor?" I stared out the window at the gathering clouds. "It's as if aliens chose to make contact by landing on our pier."

"Or Bigfoot emerged from the woods to visit the Clam Shack."

"Or the Loch Ness monster arrived to eat blueberries."

We both laughed as we got in the truck, and then Ana shrugged. "Maybe Mrs. Fairfax wants to get away from it all. You know . . . take a vacation."

I laughed. "Here? Why would she visit someplace where the most exciting thing to happen all year is the corn-shucking contest?"

The corner of Ana's mouth twitched up. "Don't forget the August clam bake. Now *that's* wicked cool."

On the drive, we saw Hollis Adams boarding up the Clam Shack, so Ana rolled down the window to holler over. A whiff of fried clam goodness seeped in right alongside the smell of pine trees and salt water. My stomach rumbled. I hadn't eaten dinner, planning instead to fill up on mini hot dogs and meatballs on a stick.

"Hey there, Hollis. How's Louise today? She still feeling pekid?"

"Ayuh. But that's to be expected when ya got a bun in the oven."

That was Maine-speak for saying that someone was going to have a baby.

Ana laughed. She'd stopped the truck smack in the middle of the empty road, but that was okay because the only time there'd been traffic in Whickett Harbor was when Mo Allen Kiser hit a moose on Main Street.

"Good thing you'll be home tonight," Ana said. "Hope the storm doesn't cause any damage." She paused. "Pop's Café staying open?"

"Only for a few more hours 'cause of all these tourists in town for the library shindig. You ask me, the library should've canceled, but Violet wouldn't hear of it."

"No way." I couldn't help myself—the words burst out.

Hollis chuckled. "That you, Jane? You look pretty tonight. How's your father?"

"Good. He's working." That went without saying.

"What grade you goin' into this year?"

"Seventh."

Hollis shook his head. "Both you and Kitty again? Miss Bates's going to have her hands full when school opens next week, ain't she?"

"Are you implying that Jane isn't a total angel?" Ana said, pretending to be offended on my behalf. "I'll have you know that someday we'll be giving Jane a cocktail party and a book reading. You mark my words."

"All right," Hollis said, but it came out sounding like *a'ight*. "Better get a move on then. Let this writer lady meet her competition." He winked and Ana threw one last lazy wave over her shoulder before she rolled up the window and stepped on the gas.

A few minutes later we reached the library.

We got out and walked slowly along the stone path and then up the cracked front steps. The library is pretty small, and tonight they had the front door open, so people spilled out onto the lawn. Classical music sounded from inside. I saw a lot of faces I recognized, but what was more incredible was that I also saw faces that I *didn't* recognize.

Genuine strangers. Lots of them.

Granny V spotted us the minute we got there and hurried over. She had on her funeral face, and for a moment my stomach sank down to my toes. Had Mrs. Fairfax canceled because of the storm? Had she mixed us up with Bar Harbor, where all the tourists go?

"Jane, I am *so* sorry," Granny V said. The *V* stood for Violet, and tonight she wore a violet dress with pearls that made her look like a fancy giant grape. "I thought you knew . . . Mrs. Fairfax said she'd do a school visit sometime during the year, but tonight is for adults only. No children allowed."

No children allowed?

My breath left in a rush and I could feel the heat creep up my neck to the tips of my ears. Discrimination!

"Couldn't you make an exception?" Ana asked. "You know Jane is a serious writer. She won't make a peep."

Granny V fluttered one hand in front of her face. "Oh dear. This is all my fault. I should have been clear. I'm afraid we can't make an exception because the library is serving *alcohol* tonight." She whispered "alcohol" as if the word alone might make us tipsy.

Ana looked at me, and I could see that she was gearing up to keep arguing, but I knew Granny V would just get more upset and then she'd get overheated, and next thing we knew she'd be having palpitations. So I shook my head and pulled Ana aside, handing her my spiral notebook.

"You have to take notes for me."

It was as if I'd asked her to pick up seagull poop with her bare hands. "Oh, Jane. I'm terrible at taking notes. I wasn't any good in school. You know I never got above a C. Besides, what will you do if I stay here?"

I shrugged. "I've got a book in the truck. I'll take it next door to Pop's Café and read until Dad picks me up." That was a lie, but I knew Ana wouldn't say yes if she thought I'd have nothing to do. "Please?"

She chewed on her bottom lip, then glanced from the truck to the library. Finally, she sighed. "Okay. Fine."

I threw my arms around her waist. "Thanks. Write down *everything*."

"I'll do my best. Tell Pop I said to keep an eye on you until your father shows up, and don't talk to any strangers." Ana scowled, but then her scowl faded and she hugged me back. "You and your dad stay safe tonight, okay? I'll come by in the morning to check in and give you my notes."

I nodded. "We'll be fine. You stay safe too."

Ana hesitated, but then she turned and disappeared into the crowd. I watched her go, a fake smile plastered on my face. Once she was gone, the smile dropped.

No children allowed?

What a stupid rule! I fingered my new necklace and thought about the quote inside. There was zero chance I was going to be banished to Pop's Café—not when I had a powerful imagination on my side. Surely I could come up with some way to hear J. E. Fairfax speak.

I left the building, then walked around to try the side door. Locked. Then I tried the staircase leading to the basement, but the gate was latched. Still, there had to be a way. I paced the perimeter looking for an entrance. The downstairs windows were open, but they were right behind the podium and I could see people milling about with their fancy drinks.

Finally, I eyed the maple tree on the side of the building. I'd climbed it before, and if I reached the top branch I knew I could open the attic window. From the top of the attic staircase it would be possible to hear everything J. E. Fairfax said without being seen.

I marched up to the tree and planted my foot against the trunk. Two tries later it was pretty clear that dress shoes and tree climbing weren't a good match, so I slipped off my shoes, leaving them on the sidewalk below, and then hitched myself up to the top branches barefoot. Luck was on my side, because the window was open, so if I leaned just the right way . . .

The branch swayed as I crawled to the end. A stick tore at the front of Kitty's dress. A sheath of bright red maple leaves knocked out the clips from my hair, but I didn't dare lift my hand to fix them. I looked down and the ground seemed a hundred feet away.

If I fell, how many bones would I break?

My heart pounded and for a split second I considered making my way back down to safety. But those unjust words echoed in my head.

No children allowed.

I gritted my teeth and leaped from the branch to the window, as graceful as a flock of turkeys scared into scrub brush. Branches snapped, and leaves fell like they'd been caught in a nor'easter. With a stomach-wrenching *ooof,* I landed half on and half off the windowsill, my legs hanging over the edge. In one dizzying moment I realized I was slipping. There's something awful about that kind of panic, as if your whole body cries out at once.

But then two strong hands grasped my forearms and pulled me in.

I landed face-first, smack on top of someone. My knee gouged the person's stomach, and I heard them say "ugh," and then "ouch," and then the same arms that had pulled me in were pushing me away so hard, I fell over backward.

"Get off me! What kind of person climbs through an attic window?"

I clambered to my feet only to come face-to-face with a boy my own age. He had short dark hair and even darker, stormy eyes. He was wearing beige pants, a sweater vest, and a paisley tie, and when he spoke, he had a British accent. He was probably the son of some tourist who was here for the event.

At first I'd felt grateful, but after he yelled at me, my gratitude turned into annoyance. My whole face went hot.

"You didn't have to help me," I said, brushing leaves off Kitty's dress. "I would've made it on my own."

"Oh really?" the boy said. "You don't think I just saved your life? Because from where I sat, it looked like you were about to get yourself killed."

The Hello Kitty face had lost a nose, whiskers, and one eye, making it look like the deranged cat from Dad's favorite Stephen King novel, *Pet Sematary*.

I wanted to be polite, but I snapped instead. "Why are you even up here? This is my spot."

"Oh? Well, I got here first." The boy's expression was pinched.

"Yes, but this is *my* library." I'd always considered the Whickett Harbor Library my second home. It was my favorite place on earth aside from my writing nook.

The boy snorted. "You're welcome to it. I'm surprised they even call this a library. It's more like a glorified closet with books in it. What do people do once they've read them all?"

My jaw clenched and despite myself, my fists balled up.

"Once we've read all the books," I said, "we write our own."

The boy laughed. "What would *you* write about? Growing up in the smallest, smelliest spot on the continent? What it's like to live in the least diverse town in America?"

It was true that almost everyone who lived here was white, and it was also true that Whickett Harbor smelled like a medley of clams, seaweed, and salt water all year round, but that didn't mean we didn't have other good qualities.

"Or maybe someone could write a book about how to throw a cocktail party with butter crackers, cheese spray, and plastic fruit decorations," the boy continued.

I scowled. "What would you know about cocktail parties anyway?"

"Plenty," he said, jutting out his chin. "I've been to more than I can count. And this is the first one where people have shown up in work boots and suspenders." He looked me up and down. "Or barefoot."

"At least I'm not wearing a tie."

The boy's ears turned red.

"Why are *you* here?" he asked. "Let me guess, you think you're going to be a writer, so you snuck in to hear all of the great J. E. Fairfax's advice."

My throat constricted. "You . . . you don't know a thing about me . . ." I sputtered. "Or Whickett Harbor! We may not be sophisticated, but at least we've got . . ."

And that's when the worst thing happened. I couldn't think of one quality Whickett Harbor had that I could boast about.

The boy waited to see if I'd come up with something, and then he laughed and sat back down where he'd made himself comfortable with a science textbook and a bottle of Joe's lemonade.

"Just like I thought," he muttered. "Hundreds of miles from home and I'm stuck in the middle of nowhere."

Even if I'd thought of a comeback, I wouldn't have spoken another word if you'd paid me a million dollars. My eyes burned with angry tears, but I was determined not to let them escape. Not in front of *him*.

I walked to the edge of the attic's spiral staircase, where I could sit with my legs dangling down. I couldn't see much from this angle, but I could hear the low murmur of voices, and when J. E. Fairfax began her speech, I'd be able to hear her perfectly. At least, I would if I could stop the angry buzzing in my ears.

That boy was mean and stuck-up. He was invading *my* sacred space, and worst of all, every single thing he'd said had been true.

CHAPTER THREE

$\mathcal{S}$taring down at the sliver of the library that I could see through the open door made me want to wither up like sea kelp in the summer sun. What if the boy was right? I'd always been proud to be from Maine. I'd been proud to claim Whickett Harbor as my home, even if it was about as isolated as a person could get. But now I couldn't help seeing us through his eyes.

There wasn't anything glamorous about Whickett Harbor. The cocktail party wasn't like parties in the movies. The space was cramped, and I could see a red Jell-O mold sitting on the librarian's desk surrounded by plastic champagne glasses and a box of wine. The desk had been covered with a tablecloth, but the tablecloth had been hand-knitted out of fishing net by Mr. Frankel, who'd donated his creation to the library. And the conversations I overheard weren't exactly sophisticated.

" . . . can't remember the last time a hurricane hit Whickett Harbor. When was it? Hurricane Bob in 1991, I think."

"Did Pat get the lobster boats tied up tight? Winds are gonna be high. We'll be getting a heck of a storm surge."

The weather. That's what people in Whickett Harbor had to talk about? Nothing was more ordinary than the weather. If I could have climbed out the window and back down the tree, I would have, but I wasn't about to let that boy know he'd gotten to me. Plus, I still held on to a ray of hope that J. E. Fairfax might say something that would teach me the secret to literary success.

Ana said she'd never met someone who wrote as much as I did, and that was a good thing, because without writing, my life would've been downright lonely. Ana spent time taking care of old Mrs. Wallace. Kitty took dance, piano, and gymnastics—all of which were over an hour's drive each way—and Dad was always at the lab.

A microphone crackled and I finally caught a glimpse of J. E. Fairfax. She was tall and beautiful with her dark hair swept up into a feathery style. She wore heels that had to be two inches high and a pantsuit that glittered with shimmering sparkles. I'd read the "About the Author" paragraph that the library had posted online, and it said that J. E. Fairfax had been born in Brazil. Her skin was a deep tan, and she had high, sharp cheekbones. She was the most beautiful woman I'd ever laid eyes on.

I dared a tiny glance over my shoulder to see if the boy was watching. Whickett Harbor might be common, but what would he think of J. E. Fairfax? Surely, he'd be impressed. But his nose was buried in the science book and he never once looked up.

Fine. I was more determined than ever to ignore him.

After what seemed like an eternity, Granny V concluded her introduction, and finally J. E. Fairfax took the microphone. The moment she opened her mouth, my world imploded. That British accent I'd heard moments before? That same accent was coming out of *her* mouth. Why did she sound British and not Brazilian?

It didn't take a genius to figure out the truth. The boy, with his perfectly styled black hair and dark, brooding eyes, was her son.

Every muscle in my body twitched as I fought the urge to turn around, but I would *not* give him the satisfaction. I tried to listen to Mrs. Fairfax's speech. I vaguely made out the words as she said how happy she was to be in Whickett Harbor. But now the whole speech was tainted. Did she really want to be here? Or would she and her son have a great time making jokes about us as soon as they left?

"The first time I visited Whickett Harbor," Mrs. Fairfax

said, "I was a young girl passing through on my way from Bar Harbor up to New Brunswick. My family's car broke down, and we ended up spending a delightful day by the seashore. I was charmed. Utterly charmed."

Behind me, the boy snorted. "Who could be charmed by this place?"

My lips pursed so tight, they hurt.

"I remember thinking that the coast of Maine was the ideal setting for a novel," J. E. Fairfax said. "Sweeping and romantic. I fell in love with the rocky coastline and the white birch trees. Even as my family moved first to London, and then to Wales, my soul craved the slower pace of life here in coastal America."

"Slower pace . . . that's one way of putting it," the boy muttered. "Try nonexistent. I bet this town hasn't changed in a hundred years."

I turned and glared. "Will you be quiet? I'm trying to listen."

"Why?" the boy asked. "She just says what her audiences want to hear. She knows all the right words, but—"

I cut him off.

"You shouldn't talk that way about your mom," I said, taking a chance that I was right about how they were related. Sure enough, his expression changed.

"My mum has more than enough people who are nice

to her. They fawn all over her. That's all she really cares about."

Although I hated to admit it, I could relate. My mother had moved from being an actress to a filmmaker, and she'd long ago chosen her career over me. Dad always said that when it came to parenting, Mom was doing the best she knew how, but one week in August, one week over Christmas break, and a gift on my birthday wasn't saying much.

I gave the boy my worst death glare. "Maybe people aren't fawning over your mother, they're giving her a little respect. Unlike her ungrateful son."

"I'm not ungrateful," he said. "I'm just telling things as they are."

"Please," I scoffed. "I bet your family is super rich and you get to travel all over the world doing incredible things, but instead of appreciating it, you moan and groan about how you'd rather stay home."

"Oh yes? Well . . ."

I could tell he didn't actually have anything to say, and it would have felt good to watch him sputter, but at that moment I heard the words I'd been waiting to hear for weeks.

"So, I'll give you my very best writing advice . . ."

The boy started to say something, but I shushed him with a sharp, sweeping hand motion. I held my breath.

What would she say? Would it be something profound? Some bit of technical knowledge that only a best-selling author would have discovered? I closed my eyes, waiting for the words that would change my life.

"Write what you know," J. E. Fairfax said.

I opened one eye. Wait. *What?*

"Each of you has been granted a wonderful, unique life," she continued, "and the insights you've gained are unlike the insights of any other person on this planet. No one else has experienced exactly what you've experienced. We all have different families, different homes . . . We grew up in different settings and see the world through our own lens. When you bring that to your writing, you will have found your true voice as an author."

Write what you know? Those were J. E. Fairfax's words of wisdom? That had to be the worst advice I'd ever heard! How in the world was I supposed to create amazing stories when all I had to draw from was boring old Whickett Harbor?

Behind me, the boy chuckled. "Disappointed? I tried to warn you."

I whirled on him. "All right, you. Listen up. If you think—"

The lights flickered. A titter of nervous laughter came

from downstairs, but then Mrs. Fairfax resumed her speech. The boy and I got up at the same time and headed to the attic window. Outside, the clouds had gotten so dark, it looked like night had fallen early. It wasn't raining yet, but the wind whipped the birch trees so hard, they bent halfway to the ground.

"Whoa," the boy breathed. He was standing right next to me, and when our pinkie fingers touched, there was a flash of lightning outside. "Have you ever been in a hurricane before?"

I shook my head. "Nope. Last one to hit Whickett Harbor came before I was born. We've gotten the outskirts of hurricanes, but I've never seen one make landfall. You?"

"Same," he said. "Wish I could see what the ocean looks like right now."

I paused. Was I about to make trouble? Perhaps. But wasn't that the only way anything exciting would ever happen for me to write about?

"You *could* see the ocean," I offered. "It's not that far. If you climbed down the tree and ran to the end of the road, you'd see the shore and the breakwater." I paused. "Of course, a boy like you would never do that, so maybe I shouldn't have said anything."

His brows made a deep V. "What's that mean? A boy like me?"

I gestured to his sweater vest. "You know . . . someone so *tidy*. I bet you've never climbed a tree in your life."

"I've climbed plenty of trees. And if you can do it wearing . . . that"—he pointed at my bedraggled *Hello Kitty* turned *Pet Sematary* dress—"then I certainly can."

"So, go ahead," I prodded. "Unless you're scared. Do proper British boys do anything daring?"

"I'm not British; I'm Welsh," he growled.

That was interesting, but since he'd been tearing down the place I lived all night, I shrugged as if I couldn't care less. This seemed to infuriate him more than anything else I'd said so far. He walked to the window, opened it all the way, and before I had a chance to take back my taunting words, he'd made a flying leap onto the tree. The whole thing happened so suddenly, I just stood there blinking as he climbed to the ground.

I never thought he'd do it!

Reality hit me like a breeching whale smacking the water. What if he'd fallen? I could've gotten J. E. Fairfax's son killed. In fact, right at this very moment, he was running down the street, heading for the one place anyone with sense knew not to go in a storm. What if he went out on the breakwater and a rogue wave pulled him in?

Me and my stupid mouth.

Down below, I could hear J. E. Fairfax taking questions

from the audience, unaware that her child was in mortal danger. I took a deep breath, trying hard not to glance at the street. Slowly, I climbed onto the windowsill and stood so my bare toes curled over the edge. I squeezed my eyes shut.

"Oh lord, oh lord, oh lord. Please don't let me die."

I flung myself at the tree. I aimed for the trunk and smacked into it before sliding down a branch or two. I caught myself in time, but not before I heard a loud tearing sound. I'd ripped a long gash in the side of Kitty's dress. Blood rose to the surface of my palms as my skin throbbed in time with my heartbeat.

"Stupid boy. What kind of person listens to some girl he doesn't even know?"

When I got to the ground I found Kitty's shoes where I'd left them and stuffed my feet into them. Then I took off running, straight down Moxie Lane.

I was so mad, I could hardly see straight. I'd gone from future *New York Times* best seller to *America's Most Wanted* in one disastrous moment. I strained for any sign of the boy, but I didn't see him.

Until I reached the breakwater.

The breakwater was constructed from a collection of huge stones, some of them the size of small cars. I wasn't sure when it had been built, but it sheltered the area where boats came and went from the local marina. The breakwater was tall, twice my father's height above the ocean's surface, and it stretched out for nearly a half mile. Some of the boulders were flat and some were rounded, and there were spots where huge gaps opened up between them. The rocks were often slippery, and people had toppled off them during storms, pulled into the churning waters and drowned before they could fight their way back to shore.

The boy was already climbing the lowest boulder.

I picked up speed. "Hey! Stop!"

He wasn't that far from me, but my voice was carried away by the wind that whipped against me, lashing my face. He'd taken off his tie, so he looked like any other boy now, and I was sorry I'd ever been so angry at him.

"Hey," I called again. "Stop!"

This time he heard me and slid down to the sandy beach.

"You shouldn't go out there," I hollered over the wind. "The breakwater is dangerous in a storm." I'd been running so fast, it was hard to catch my breath. I bent over, leaning my scraped hands on my knees. "What were you thinking?" I demanded. "Your mother is probably panicking by now."

The boy laughed a dry, bitter laugh. "Mum didn't even know I was there. I was supposed to leave with my older sister, but she's a prat and I'm tired of Caroline being in charge all the time, so I stayed and snuck upstairs."

"What about your dad?"

"My parents got divorced."

"Oh."

"Besides," the boy said, "no matter what punishment I get, it will be totally worth it. I mean, look at the ocean! It's incredible!"

He was right. The sky was a solid gray, and the waves frothed with a deafening roar. Sea spray filled the air with every slap of the surf against the boulders.

We were silent, in awe of the scene before us.

It *was* beautiful. In all my life, I'd never seen the ocean look quite like this. Not a single boat was in sight. There weren't even any seagulls in the sky, just roiling clouds that looked like they might burst at any moment. We stood there for a long time, too transfixed to move.

"Guess we should go back," the boy said at last, yelling over the howling wind.

I nodded, still watching the waves. As if on cue, the first splatters of rain hit my face. I'd have thought the boy might panic, but he'd gone back to staring at some spot far past the horizon. Was Wales across the ocean from here? Did he miss it?

"Hey," I said at last, "what's your name anyway?"

"Devon," he said. "What's yours?"

"Jane."

"Let's go," he said. "Before anyone misses us."

Unfortunately, we were already too late for that.

CHAPTER FOUR

The first sign of trouble was the darkness. When we finally reached the library in the brutal, pelting rain, the lights were off and the entire parking lot was empty. Had we been away that long? Or had the power gone out and they'd closed up early? A sinking feeling made my chest tight.

Behind me, I heard Devon curse and he darted forward to pull at the library door. Of course it didn't budge. He swirled to face me and his eyes were huge. "You!" he said, shouting over the rain and wind. "This is all your fault. We're locked out!"

"Me? I'm not the one who jumped out the window."

"I never would have left the library if you hadn't goaded me into it."

"You could have said no. It was just a stupid dare."

"Well, you were the one who—"

We were interrupted by a gust of wind so strong, it blew

the library's metal trash cans over with a loud crash. They rolled across the lawn and banged into a lamppost.

"Come on," I said. "We better walk to my friend Ana's place before the storm gets any worse."

Ana's apartment wasn't far, but my feet hurt from sliding around in Kitty's too-big flats. Blisters were forming on my heels. We trudged past the Clam Shack, the town hall, and the post office before reaching the small houses at the end of Main Street.

I wasn't too worried yet; I could always count on Ana.

Except, I didn't see Ana's truck in the driveway. She and Mrs. Wallace shared a duplex. I banged on Ana's door as Devon hunched beside me. No answer. Even though it was August, the temperature had dropped and I couldn't stop shivering.

I knocked again, louder this time. Still no response.

"She's probably next door with Mrs. Wallace," I offered, but even as I said those words, I knew that if Ana were there, I'd see her truck.

Devon was already knocking, yelling, "Hello!" and "Open up!" But Mrs. Wallace was almost completely deaf, and if Ana were there, she'd have answered.

"Now what?" Devon asked. "Try another house?"

The downpour showed no sign of easing up. I chewed my

bottom lip, shading my face. "We could try some of the other homes on Main Street, but I know the Jackmans evacuated to their daughter's place inland and the Reeds have gone for the season. I'm sure the Adamses are around—they own the Clam Shack—but they live nearly a mile away."

"Have I mentioned this is all your fault?" Devon asked.

I ignored him. "Our best bet is to go straight to the police station. We'll explain everything and Josh can bring us home in his truck. Simple."

Then why was my pulse racing? I had to take three deep breaths to get my breathing back to normal.

"There's nothing simple about being stranded outside in the middle of nowhere during a hurricane," Devon snapped.

"We aren't in the middle of nowhere. We're in Whickett Harbor. A thriving, mini-metropolis."

My words might have been more convincing if every building in sight hadn't been boarded up or abandoned. There weren't even any vehicles on the road.

My shoulders slumped. "Let's go."

Ten minutes later we reached the police station, but the door was locked. The rain beat relentlessly against my skin and the wind made a noise that could have come from a slasher movie. A sign was posted in the window that read: ALL UNITS OUT ON CALL.

"All units out on call?" Devon said. "But there's a hurricane! What if someone needs them?"

I glared. "That's why they're out on call, Einstein." I didn't mention that we only *had* two units—Officer Josh Tate and Officer Deb Cote.

"Now what?" Devon squeaked. "We're going to die out here! We're going to get brain damage from a falling tree limb or we'll be washed away in a flash flood or die of hypothermia."

He said something in Welsh that was either a prayer or a curse. I took him by the shoulders and shook him hard.

"Get ahold of yourself. We're not going to die. We're going to . . ." What the heck were we going to do? "We'll go back to the library and wait for someone to find us. We'll climb back in the same way we went out."

"You want to climb a tree in this wind? Are you insane?!" Devon waved to indicate the pine trees on both sides of the road that were bent low, their branches stretched taut against the gale. Suddenly, with a spine-tingling *crack,* one of the tallest pines split down the middle, crashing across the street. The top branches landed within spitting distance from us, and I screamed so loud, my throat got sore. I'd never been so scared in my entire life.

"Run!" I hollered.

We sprinted toward the library, my blisters burning, only to find that someone had shut the attic window and propped a board against the inside. I could see the wood behind the glass.

"I'm too young to die," Devon moaned.

I shook my head. There was only one thing to do. I picked up the largest rock I could find, feeling its cold weight in my hand, and walked straight up to the front door.

I, Jane Brannen, was about to become a vandal of the very worst sort. A library vandal. But this was a matter of life and death. I hurled the rock through the bottom square of glass and squeezed my eyes shut as the pane shattered.

I heard Devon's startled yelp beside me. "You're out of your mind. I've been stranded with a crazy girl. You're probably related to Stephen King, aren't you?"

"Be. Quiet. Give me your sweater vest."

"Why?" Devon's eyes looked even huger than before, but he peeled it off his soaking body and handed it to me. I wrapped it around my hand and forearm as I reached through the jagged glass to unlock the door.

Finally, the lock snicked open and I freed my arm. Devon and I dashed inside, then pulled the door closed behind us. We stood in place, dripping on the floor mat, breathing hard.

"You're welcome," I said at last.

"We could still die of hypothermia," Devon said.

I threw my hands up. Impossible boy!

"I'm going to look down here for something dry to change into. You can look through the costumes in the attic." I debated withholding my additional knowledge, but decided to share if only to stop his whining. "And there are cookies and grape juice in the kitchen. I'm pretty sure no one ever died while eating cookies and drinking grape juice."

This time Devon said nothing. I found a flashlight in the kitchen and gave it to him, then watched as his beam of light bounced up the attic steps. I stumbled back into the dark kitchen and sorted through the clothes hanging behind the door. There were two coats, a leftover winter scarf no one had ever claimed, and as I'd expected, one of Granny V's dresses that she kept there in case of emergency spills and splatters. Every inch of me was sopping wet and freezing cold. I needed to get dry.

I took the dress into the library bathroom and stripped off all my wet clothes. There was one crocheted hand towel next to the sink, and I used it to dry off, then pulled the dress over my head. Granny V is a large woman with a huge bosom, so the dress sagged straight down to my toes. I looked like I was wearing a floor-length purple bag.

My one saving grace was that when I stepped out of

the bathroom, Devon came down the stairs from the attic dressed as a scarecrow, straight down to the faux straw collar. I couldn't help it. I laughed until tears rolled down my cheeks.

"Oh, and you think you look good?" Devon snapped. "You look like a giant purple marshmallow after it's been held over the fire and started to melt."

"Whatever." I wiped my eyes on my sleeve. "Let's get something to eat."

Turns out there was more than just cookies and grape juice in the library. All of the food from the cocktail party had been left on the table. My guess was that when the power went out, they'd decided to leave everything, close up early, and deal with the leftovers the next day. That was excellent for me, because I was starving. My stomach growled loudly.

I grabbed a handful of mini hot dogs wrapped in crescent rolls and started eating. When those were gone, I helped myself to a tiny quiche.

"Don't mind if I do," I said, sampling the quiche. Then I spit it into a napkin. "Bleh. Spinach."

Devon's mouth hung open. "You have the manners of a barbarian."

"Oh? And I ought to be polite for *your* sake?" Locking eyes with him, I grabbed a canister of fake cheese spray and squirted some into my open mouth.

Devon's face was a mask of horror.

"It's good," I said, smacking my lips. "You should try it before you judge."

"Never."

"Just try it." I grabbed his hand and aimed the nozzle so I could squirt the cheese onto his finger, but he jerked back and the bright yellow goop ended up all over the front of his scarecrow costume. Devon didn't even hesitate. He grabbed the nacho-flavored canister and squirted it into my hair.

"Jerk!" I hollered. I grabbed a handful of Jell-O mold and lobbed it at him.

"Brat!"

A fistful of crumbled Ritz crackers rained over my head.

"Animal!"

I stuck a mini meatball down Devon's collar.

"Spanner!"

He upended an entire bowl of potato chips down Granny V's dress.

"Snob!"

I grabbed a deviled egg and smooshed it into his face.

We might have gone through the entire table of finger foods if the library door hadn't flung open at that exact moment. A flashlight beam illuminated the scene, and I froze with my hand in midair, still clutching a squishy white egg cup.

"Jane Sylvia Brannen!"

You know you're in trouble when you hear your full name. But you're beyond trouble when you hear your full name growled by the town sheriff. Usually, Joshua Tate was a cuddly bear who picked me up and twirled me in circles, but not today.

"What on earth are you kids doing? Half the town is out looking for you! We've all been worried sick, and you're in here—" He gestured to the mess we'd made.

"I can explain," I started, but Josh cut me off. He brought his walkie-talkie to his mouth, pressed the button, and spoke into it. "Emmett? Ana? I found 'em. They're at the library."

My father's voice crackled over the speaker. *"But we already checked the library."*

"Ayuh. Must have doubled back."

"Ten-four," Ana said. *"I'll tell the others."* She paused. *"Emmett, I'm sure there's a good explanation."*

Ana always had my back, no matter what, but looking around at the mess we'd made, I couldn't say her faith in me was justified this time. Beside me, Devon shifted nervously from one foot to the other.

"I better return to Mrs. Wallace. She'll be clenched tighter than a clam at high tide," Ana's voice said over the speaker.

"I'll wait here until you arrive, Emmett," Josh said, "and then I'll take the boy home. His family is frantic. It was all I could do to keep his mom from driving around in her sports car to look for him."

"Ten-four."

Josh hooked the walkie-talkie back on his belt and opened his mouth to say something, but Devon beat him to it.

"Was my mother really going to look for me?"

"Of course," Josh said. "I told her she'd get herself killed driving around in that silly little car in a hurricane, but she still fought me." He took a deep breath. "Now, what in tarnation happened?"

Both Devon and I started talking at once, until finally Josh shook his head. "All right, all right. I've heard enough. Why don't you two clean up the mess you've made while we're waiting for Emmett?"

Devon wiped deviled egg off his cheek. I finger-combed crackers out of my hair. Then we both set to work picking up food and depositing it in the trash can. Josh watched us for a moment, and then he cleared his throat.

"You should know, Jane, that your mother called in the midst of all this. Right before the phone lines went down. She wanted to check up on you and make sure you were safe, but we got cut off right after I told her that you were missing, and now there's no way to reach her until service is restored."

My stomach plummeted. Without saying as much, Josh was letting me know that I'd done something far worse than mess up the library carpet. He'd been Dad's best friend since their school days, and he was my godfather, so he knew that for the past few months, Mom had been making noises about me needing to expand my horizons. Lately every conversation with her was laced with things like "You need to see the world, Jane," and "You're getting older now. Don't you think it's time you got out of Whickett Harbor?"

Mom said "Whickett Harbor" like it was a curse word.

I pursed my lips and wouldn't let myself cry. Not in front of Devon. We both worked steadily, throwing away the leftover food and getting down on our knees to wash the carpet with wet paper towels. Neither of us made eye contact and Josh didn't say another word.

I was so busy cleaning, I didn't hear when my father arrived. Before I knew it, I was in his arms, scooped off the floor, and he was squeezing me so tight, I couldn't breathe.

"Don't ever scare me like that again," Dad said.

Josh came over and clapped him on the shoulder. "I'll take the boy home now that you're here."

Dad nodded. He looked me up and down, frowning. "I don't even want to know what you're wearing. Where's Kitty's dress?"

"In the kitchen. I'll get it," I said.

When I came back, dress in hand, Dad said, "Let's go. You can explain yourself later."

Devon retrieved his wet clothes, then followed Josh out of the library. The wind was so strong, it nearly blew them sideways. Josh motioned for us to follow, and when we did, I was hit by a gust that would have knocked me off my feet if Dad didn't have hold of my arm. The four of us pressed against the gale force winds to reach the two trucks in the parking lot.

Even if I'd wanted to say goodbye, I couldn't have. The wind roared like a banshee. Dad pushed me into the cab and slammed the door shut. I watched as Josh's headlights lit up the deep gray sheets of rain and his truck pulled out and drove away.

I wondered if I'd ever see that annoying boy again.

Dad hadn't said a word, but I recognized the hard set of his jaw. He backed his truck out and kept his eyes fixed on the road as he drove, swerving as branches blew in our path and clutching the steering wheel so tightly, his knuckles turned white. I knew that underneath his concentration, something else was lurking.

My father was afraid, and it wasn't entirely because of the storm.

CHAPTER FIVE

*I*t took a lot to make my father angry. Usually, he was the most easygoing person around, but when his temper did flare up, he got stone-cold quiet. Once, he'd seen someone dumping garbage onto the beach and he'd been so furious, he'd hollered at them. After they'd driven away, he hadn't said a word for two hours straight.

Tonight, he didn't speak until we'd made it back home. Our power was out and the house was dark, but I could still make out Dad's angry expression in the dim light.

"So," he said at last, "I've been able to piece together some of the story thanks to Ana. You weren't allowed to go to the author shindig, but instead of going to Pop's Café like she told you to, you snuck back into the library. I'm guessing that's where you met that boy?"

I nodded.

"Was it his idea to go wandering around town?"

Maybe I could've lied right then, but Dad and I didn't lie

to each other. We were a team, and that meant telling the truth.

"No. It was my fault," I admitted. "I kind of tricked him into going out, and then once he'd done it, I had to make him come back, so I followed after him. But then . . ."

My voice trailed off and Dad frowned.

"I'm sorry," I said. "I'll do anything to make things right."

"Yes, you will," Dad agreed. "I'm not sure what that will look like, but we're both going to sleep on it and come up with something in the morning. Understood?"

I nodded.

"All right," Dad said. "Head on up and get out of that silly dress. We'll have to get it dry-cleaned before we return it to Violet. And that cost, along with the cost of buying Kitty a new dress, will come out of your allowance."

"Okay." I knew Kitty would forgive me for ruining her dress, especially if it gave her an excuse to shop for a new one.

I moved toward the stairs, but Dad reached out and pulled me close once more. He pressed his cheek against my hair. "Lord almighty, I was scared, Jane. If I ever lost you . . ."

Dad's whole body trembled, and I held him tight.

"You won't lose me," I promised. "I won't ever let that happen."

Dad breathed in. "You better not," he said. "'Cause I love you more than lobster, and that's saying a lot."

I laughed a small, tired laugh. "Yeah, but do you love me more than plankton?"

This time Dad made a face. "Whoa, now that's asking too much!"

"Dad," I complained.

He gave me a shove toward the staircase. I was halfway up before he said, "I love you more than *everything*."

Upstairs in my tiny bedroom with the sloping ceiling, I peeled out of Granny V's dress with the food stains down the front. I took off the necklace Ana had given me and set it carefully on my dresser, and then I got into my oldest, softest pajamas, and wrapped myself in my worn patchwork quilt. I had a chill I couldn't shake, and the noise of the hurricane was loud and unrelenting.

I tossed and turned. Sometime later a branch smacked hard against my window and I jolted upright. Our entire house groaned in protest.

Dad and I live in a house we call the B&B. It dates back to 1896, and it's crooked and sprawling—two stories, three bathrooms, and five bedrooms—and everyone who visits says the exact same thing: "You should turn this place into a bed and breakfast!"

They're right, except for two glaring problems. First, Whickett Harbor has a population of 876 and hardly anyone visits. Second, Dad would make the world's worst host. *Bed? Sure, you're welcome to stay, so long as you don't mind unwashed sheets. Breakfast? You mean we're out of milk, bread, and cereal, again? Oh well. Help yourself to anything you can find, just don't open any little glass jars!*

So far, our house had lasted over a hundred years, but that night it didn't seem sturdy enough to withstand the storm. I was used to the creaking floorboards and the cracks in the walls, but now the frame groaned and the wind battered the house so hard, I thought it might collapse.

It was hours before I finally fell asleep.

When I woke up to sunlight streaming through my window, I felt as if someone had torn away a veil. The world was bright and vivid again, and the hurricane seemed like a distant memory. Devon's mad dash to the breakwater. The tree falling across the road. Josh bursting into the library. None of that seemed real on this perfect blue-sky morning in Maine.

Only my impending talk with Dad made the night's events seem like more than a dream. My father's usual idea of discipline was to take me for a ride in his old truck and to say in his most somber voice, "Jane, I am mighty disappointed in you." Some people might think there ought to be more to it than that—but for me, Dad's mighty disappointment was consequence enough.

Just as I'd expected, as soon as we were done with breakfast, Dad said, "Jane, let's go for a ride."

We piled into the truck and he was quiet again, staring out the window. We drove around Whickett Harbor surveying the damage, and I knew he wanted me to understand how close Devon and I had come to getting seriously hurt. Several fishing boats had been cast on shore, trees were down all around town, the roof of the Lobster Wharf had blown off, and some of the other shops had broken windows. Debris was scattered everywhere.

When we rounded the corner onto Moxie Lane, we saw Ana out with the volunteer firehouse crew, cutting up a fallen pine. Ana was petite, but today she looked even smaller than usual compared to the huge tree in front of her. She was dressed in leg protectors and a flannel shirt with thick, elbow-length leather gloves, and her long blond hair was pulled back under a kerchief. When she saw Dad's truck she set down the chain saw and stood with her hands on her hips.

Dad pulled over and we both got out. I waited to see how angry Ana would be on a scale of one to ten, but the very first thing she did was hug me so hard, I thought I might pop.

"Jane Brannen," she said, "you really outdid yourself this time. Do you know how worried we were? You told me you'd go to Pop's Café, but you lied. We. Do. Not. Lie. To. Each. Other." Ana gestured between me and her and Dad. "You know better, and if it were up to me, I'd say you shouldn't be allowed near that library for a solid month."

She meant that as a hint to Dad. Ana had a habit of suggesting things in a way that would allow my father to think it had been his idea. I swallowed hard. We didn't have enough money for me to buy books online, and there wasn't a bookstore for miles around, so the library was my reading lifeline. What would I do without any new books for an entire month?

I knew that I deserved whatever punishment I got. I glanced at Dad to see whether he'd take the bait, but he was looking at Ana the way he did sometimes, kind of half shy and half confused, like he was thinking about something he couldn't make up his mind about.

Ana sighed. "I'm so glad she's safe, Emmett." She reached out and gave my father's hand a small squeeze.

"I'll make sure Jane earns the money to pay for that window," Dad said, not quite taking Ana up on her idea. But for Dad, that was still pretty strict.

"I'll pay back every penny," I said. "I promise."

"And you'll write an apology letter to the library staff," Ana said. This time it wasn't a suggestion.

I nodded. "I will. A good one. The best letter they've ever gotten."

Ana laughed. "Don't get carried away, Jane," she said. "This doesn't need to be some sweeping, dramatic tome. You just need to write a letter. A sincere one."

"I'll write the most sincere letter those librarians have ever read."

Ana turned to my father. "Did you get in touch with Susan?"

Susan is my mom. Dad winced. "No. I tried to call this morning as soon as we got power, but I got her voicemail. I'll try again," Dad offered. He pulled out his cell phone and frowned. "Aaanny minute now."

Ana kicked him with the steel toe of her boot. "Don't be a coward, Emmett Brannen." She shook her head and picked up the chain saw. "I better get back to work. Lots of trees are still down. See you two later."

"Bye, Ana." I waved, then climbed into the truck cab. I knew Dad was itching to get to the lab to check on his samples, but it would be a while before the roads were entirely cleared. Now if only cell phone service weren't available . . .

He handed me his phone and raised one eyebrow.

"Fine." I dialed Mom's number as Dad pulled back onto the road. I hit the speaker button and the sound of her voicemail message filled the truck. Mom had a special *I'm-so-cool-you-bore-me* tone she used with her colleagues in the movie business. Her message sounded as if receiving a call was a huge imposition.

"This is Susan. Leave a message if you must."

I looked at Dad. "Must I?" He chuckled under his breath.

I spoke after the beep. "Hi Mom. It's Jane. Just trying again to reach you. Wanted to let you know that I'm perfectly fine. Really great. Call me back and we can . . . talk about how great I am."

Okay. So that hadn't come out exactly right. I ended the call and Dad snorted.

"How great are you?" he teased.

"I'm so great, even I want to be me," I boasted.

"Oh yeah? Well, I'm so great, I'm jealous of myself."

"Really?" I shot back. "I'm so great, I eat soup with chopsticks."

Dad snorted. "I'm so great that when I cross the street, the cars look both ways."

We both cracked up. They were all stupid Chuck Norris jokes that Dad had found on the Internet one rainy afternoon, but we never got tired of quoting them. We traded *I'm so great* lines right up until the moment we pulled up to our house.

And then we stopped laughing.

My mother was waiting in the driveway.

CHAPTER SIX

"*M*om?" I managed to open the truck door and slide out of the cab.

Mom was here.

She'd actually come to Whickett Harbor.

She rushed up, threw her arms around me, and burst into tears. "Jane!" She cried in huge, hiccupping gulps.

"What are you doing here?" I couldn't help blurting the question out.

Mom opened her mouth to answer, but before she got a chance we were interrupted by a man coming around the side of the house. He was as tall as Dad, muscular, and he had light brown hair with too much product in it.

"Honey," he said to Mom, "I tried the back door, but I don't think—oh, hello. This must be Jane."

"Who's he?" I asked, my stomach twisting. At some point Dad had gotten out of the truck and now he'd put his hands on my shoulders. The weight of them was comforting.

Mom paused. "Well . . . you see . . . I . . . this is . . . uh, Erik." She paused. "Erik, meet Jane and Emmett."

Erik came up beside Mom and thrust out his hand for Dad to shake. Then he bent down to me, resting his palms on his knees.

"Hello there, Jane. Aren't you a pretty little girl! You look just like your mom."

Mom and I both have blue eyes and black hair, but unlike me, she actually styles hers. I wanted to kick him in the shin, but Dad squeezed my shoulders.

"Mom," I said, "why is he with you? And why did you come all the way here? I left you a message saying I'm fine. See?" I gestured to my completely intact body.

My mother cleared her throat, and then she smiled the way she did when she knew I wasn't going to like what she had to say.

"Actually, Jane . . . we were planning to visit you soon anyway, and then when you were missing, I got so worried . . ." She turned to Erik and he nodded encouragingly. "Erik suggested we book tickets on the first available flight, which was a red-eye, so we flew into Portland overnight, got a rental, and voila!"

She did a little dance step and struck a pose.

Erik laughed. "Thank goodness the airport was open. We were worried, but fortunately Portland is far enough inland that they didn't get hit. The drive here was pretty crazy, though. I had to take a million detours, and—"

I interrupted. "Why were you planning a visit?"

Mom and Erik exchanged glances. Mom looked nervous, but Erik nodded again. A big grin spread across his plastic-looking face. He had the straightest, whitest teeth I'd ever seen.

"Erik has been curious to see where I grew up, and we have some special news that we want to share with you in person." Mom stuck out her hand.

On her finger was the biggest diamond ring I'd ever seen. Apparently, Erik was rich. "Ta-da!"

In the decade since Mom had left me and Dad to go to Hollywood, she'd had fourteen different addresses, four different career paths, and at least a dozen boyfriends.

But this was the first fiancé.

"Congratulations," Dad offered.

I didn't say a word.

"Jane?" Mom prompted.

Dad nudged me and I mumbled the word *congratulations*.

"I can't wait to get to know you, Jane," Erik said. "We're going to be a family! Isn't that exciting?"

Listening to Erik speak to me as if I were a toddler made me want to puke. Exciting? Try nauseating.

"Who knows?" Erik continued. "You might be spending

a lot more time with us now that your mom and I are settling down on my estate. I've always wanted kids."

Mom cringed. "Erik—"

I could already feel the tears pooling behind my eyes, but then Erik said the one thing that could have made the situation worse.

"Oh, and someone left your mail on your front step without even putting it in a box or anything." Erik frowned as if this were the craziest thing he'd ever encountered, then waved a plain white envelope in front of my face. "Looks like a letter came for a Ms. Jane Brannen from a certain magazine! Your mom told me that you submitted your first short story for publication."

I gasped. *Mom had told him?* That was supposed to be a secret!

Erik carried on, oblivious. "That is so awesome. Susan and me . . . we can give you some great writing tips. If this is an acceptance letter we'll go out to celebrate. How about that, huh?"

I'd been waiting weeks for this letter. *Girl Power* magazine published a short story from one of their readers every month, and I was determined to get in. Even though everyone was staring at me, I couldn't help it. I tore open the envelope.

Dear Jane,

Thank you for sending "Two Princesses of Penmore" for our review. Although we loved your creativity and imagination, unfortunately we've decided to pass on publishing your work. Girl Power *receives over two hundred stories every month from girls across America, and since we publish only one work of fiction in each issue, we're forced to make difficult choices.*

Please feel free to submit new work in the future. We wish you all the best.

Sincerely,

The Editorial Team

In pen someone had scrawled: *Your writing shows potential. Keep in mind that many of* Girl Power*'s readers are older teens, so princess stories might seem too young for them. We're looking for stories that are relevant to today's modern readers.*

My heart stopped. My writing was irrelevant? I burst into tears.

"Jane—" Mom said, and then Erik said something that sounded like an apology, but I ran inside, slammed the door behind me, climbed the rickety steps to my bedroom, and flung myself on top of my old patchwork quilt.

I don't know how long it was before I heard my father's

work boots clomping along the floorboards. Then the bed sank low and his strong hand stroked my back in soothing circles.

"Aww, sprite." Dad sighed. "Sorry about the rejection letter. You'll get in next time. I know you will."

Sure. He had to say that because he was my dad.

"I know that's not all that's bothering you," Dad continued. "It was a shock to see your mom today . . . and her . . . fiancé."

My sobbing doubled.

"Your mother . . ." Dad stopped, then tried again. "Your mom and Erik . . . they shouldn't have sprung that news on you so soon. Would have been nice if they'd come in and had some coffee, asked about the hurricane cleanup, checked if you were prepared for school on Monday . . . but that's never been your mother's way. She's always been impulsive, and that's not likely to change. Still, she loves you the best she knows how, and she wants you to give her a chance."

"A chance for what? To steal me away?"

"No one's taking you away," Dad said. His voice was firm, but the only reason Mom didn't get joint custody the first time around was because she didn't ask for it. She'd decided to move to California, so it wasn't as if I could shuffle back and forth on weekends. Now, however, things might look different. Dad was still a bachelor living in a backwoods town fighting to get grants to fund his research, and some judge might think I ought to try living with Mom and her rich husband.

"Dad," I choked out, "there's no other choice. You have to get married, we need to move into a better house, and you need a more secure job. Right away."

Dad's forehead wrinkled. "Wait. What?"

I wiped my nose on my sleeve. "It's the only way to show that you're just as stable as Mom."

Dad's eyebrows shot up to the top of his forehead. "We're not moving, my job *is* secure, and I'm *not* getting married." He took a deep breath and closed his eyes. "Could we back up to the part where we were talking about your mother?"

I shrugged. As far as I was concerned, there was nothing left to say.

"She and Erik are staying for a while," Dad told me. "Apparently, he's a movie director and he's between shoots, and she's working on a new script, so they've rented the cabin down by the pier."

I groaned. "How long?"

"Three weeks."

"Three weeks?!" I burst into a whole new flood of tears. "Does she realize school starts next week?"

Dad shrugged. "She wants to bond. With you. And Erik."

"As a family?" I plucked a tissue from the box beside my bed and blew my nose. "Dad, he looks like a Ken doll."

The corner of Dad's mouth quirked up, but then he shook his head. "And since when do we judge people based on what they look like?"

"Since never?"

"That's right. Three weeks, sprite. You can make it that long. Then they'll head back to California and things will return to normal."

How could Dad miss what was right in front of his face?

After all these years my mother had finally returned to Whickett Harbor with a wealthy, sophisticated fiancé who wanted a family.

Me and Dad? We were doomed.

CHAPTER SEVEN

$\mathcal{A}$ll I wanted to do was talk to Kitty, curl up on her bed, and add a new chapter to the story we'd been creating. In this chapter, my wicked mother would turn up out of nowhere with an evil fiancé. The two princesses of Penmore would think they were friendly at first, but they'd turn out to be enemies and get taken down by the team of modern-day knights who worked to protect the heiress of the Hello Kitty fortune.

Unfortunately for me, our story would have to wait. Kitty was away for the weekend, school shopping in Meryton with one of Granny V's cousins. Since neither my father nor Granny V allowed us to have cell phones, I'd been reduced to one pathetic landline call to convey the horrible turn of events that was about to ruin my life forever.

Kitty had gasped in all the right places and sworn we'd have a sleepover as soon as she got back, but it wasn't the same as being able to make a batch of cookies and pour out my troubles over warm, melted chocolate chips.

Worse yet, I'd had to spend Sunday having the world's most awkward getting-to-know-you brunch with Mom, Dad, and Erik. Mom had insisted we drive an hour away to a fancy restaurant in Redmond even though she must have known that it was out of Dad's price range. Dad had forgotten to wear nice shoes and the hostess almost didn't let him in with his muddy work boots. There was nothing on the menu that I wanted to eat, and both Mom and Erik spent the entire meal talking about themselves.

Dad talked about an article he'd had published in the *Journal of Plankton Research* about controlling harmful cyanobacterial blooms as our climate becomes more extreme. When that topic produced only glazed expressions, he'd tried making jokes instead.

What do you carry a load of plankton in? A whale barrow.

Dad had laughed uproariously.

I'd been stuck in the middle, the only kid in the entire restaurant.

As far as I was concerned, the school year couldn't start fast enough.

∾∾∾

By the time Monday arrived, I'd never been more grateful for the first day of school. Dad dropped me off, and all around me kids were talking and laughing, but I couldn't quite shake off my weekend.

Kitty was cheerful, pirouetting across the classroom when Miss Bates called us to Culinary Arts. Our classes were mixed with three grades studying together in one room. I was relieved not to be in the youngest group this year. Kitty was too.

"This is going to be the best year ever," she said. "We're no longer sixth years, but we don't have all the pressure of the eighth years. No boring orientation stuff to go over, and we get to start using the school laptops for research projects. Best of all, no more snide remarks from Joanie Allen."

Joanie had moved up to the high school classroom. All last year she'd called us plain Jane and itty, bitty Kitty, and she'd made fun of us because neither me nor Kitty had kissed a boy yet. Good riddance.

I wanted to be as optimistic as Kitty about this year, but I couldn't pull it off. Even from afar, Mom and Erik were ruining my mood.

"It's going to be a terrible year," I moaned. "We have Miss Bates. Again."

Our school had kindergarten to twelfth grade all in the

same building, and it was so small that they combined grades. We would be stuck with the long-winded Miss Bates for three years in a row.

"True," Kitty said, "but she's nice, and even having boring Miss Bates is better than going to school in California without your very best friend. Can you imagine living without your father and Ana?" Kitty shook her head. "If your mom even breathes the word *custody,* I'll—"

She stopped. That was the problem. What *would* we do?

"Maybe she won't," I said. "She's never wanted custody before." I paused. "But she's also never come back to Whickett Harbor. And she's never had a fiancé who wants kids."

Kitty's eyes filled with tears. "Jane, what would I do if you had to move? I can't lose you too."

One of Kitty's biggest fears was losing the people she had left in her life. She'd already lost her parents, and Granny V was getting old. If I left . . .

"You won't lose me," I said. "Maybe my mother isn't even interested in custody. Maybe she really was worried about me when she heard I was missing on the night of the hurricane. Plus she wanted to introduce me to Erik. At brunch he kept saying how he wants to shoot a movie here someday."

Kitty laughed. "Wouldn't it be crazy if *they* wanted to move *here*?"

She said this as if it were a joke, but my blood ran cold.

Was that even a possibility?

All the color must have drained from my face, because Kitty's laughter petered out. "I wasn't serious, Jane. Your mother can't stand Whickett Harbor. She wouldn't move back here in a million years."

I coughed out a laugh. "Yeah. You're right. I'm worrying too much."

"Yup. You are." It was hard to keep Kitty's mood down for long. She was naturally irrepressible. "So let's get back to how awesome this year is going to be, starting right now."

Kitty spun on the toes of her brand-new pink Converse sneakers.

"Kitty," I groaned, "you're making me motion sick."

"Girls," Miss Bates said, her tone stern. "Focus." She glared at us for a moment before she went back to lecturing the sixth years about classroom rules.

Kitty picked up a wooden spoon and set it into a glass bowl, trying to look busy. She didn't like cooking. According to Kitty, fashion models didn't eat, let alone cook. I liked cooking well enough, but today I had other priorities.

"So, I've been thinking that my dad should start dating."

Kitty paused. "Really? Why?"

"Well, it doesn't seem fair that Mom has a fiancé and Dad hasn't gone on a single date in a decade. Plus, I know my mother, and she'll be less apt to push Dad around if he's got someone else on his side. Erik kept making these comments about Dad being a bachelor trying to raise a teenage daughter *all alone*."

"We're not teenagers yet," Kitty pointed out.

"No, but we will be soon, and Mom and Erik acted like Dad won't know how to raise me. Like, somehow, once I turn thirteen, I'd need my mother more than I'd need him."

Kitty scoffed. "That's ridiculous."

"I know. But it might shut them up if Dad had someone in his life."

"True," Kitty said, "but if that woman is going to compete with your mom's fiancé, then she'd have to be rich, sophisticated, and have a better job than a Hollywood film director. Good luck finding someone like that in Whickett Harbor."

I frowned. "Plus, she'd have to like science, right?"

Kitty shrugged. "Probably."

We both fell silent, pondering the odds that were stacked against us. I checked the milk to make sure it smelled okay and Kitty chewed on one of her fingernails.

"What about Ms. Lillian?" she asked. "She's not rich, but she's smart."

Ms. Lillian had been our teacher three years ago. She was nice, but I sure wouldn't want to live with her.

"Kitty, Ms. Lillian is a grandmother."

"So? She's got a PhD."

"In English literature, not science."

"What about one of the people your father works with?"

"They're all married. Or . . . strange."

Some of my father's colleagues were even weirder than him.

I sighed and walked to the refrigerator for the egg carton. I carried it to the counter, then opened the carton and took out one large brown egg. It was smooth and cold in my hand.

Writers needed to use all of their senses, so I shook the egg next to my ear.

A quiet slosh.

I lifted the egg to my nose and gave it a good sniff.

Smells like the inside of a refrigerator.

I turned my back and darted out my tongue.

Nothing.

I tried again, this time taking a good long lick. Turns out that eggshells didn't actually taste like anything.

I was so busy inspecting my egg that I wasn't paying attention to the low hum of voices and activity around me. I jumped when Mrs. Godfrey, our principal, cleared her throat to make an announcement. Somehow, she'd made her way into the middle of our classroom without my noticing and now she was standing just a few feet away from the kitchen area with a boy on either side of her.

One of them was Devon.

Had he just watched me lick an egg? Why in the world was he here at my school? Shouldn't Devon Fairfax and his family be long gone by now?

I narrowed my eyes and Devon's eyes narrowed in return.

Mrs. Godfrey cleared her throat. "Attention sixth, seventh, and eighth graders! I'd like you to welcome two new students into your midst." She forced both boys to step forward. "May I introduce Devon and Matthew Fairfax. Their mother is the author J. E. Fairfax, and they've just moved here from England."

Moved? Here?

"Wales," Devon corrected, frowning as if being introduced were a huge imposition.

Mrs. Godfrey looked blank. "Exactly." She nodded. "That's what I said."

Devon pursed his lips. Both he and his brother were wearing tan slacks with blue sport coats and bright red ties, and they looked ridiculous. No one in Whickett Harbor wore a sport coat and tie. Not even the mayor.

"Perhaps at some point you boys could give us a report about your country," Mrs. Godfrey suggested. "I'm sure everyone would be delighted to learn more about Great Britain."

The shorter boy, Matthew, smiled politely, but Devon glowered. "Wales," he repeated.

Mrs. Godfrey continued as if he hadn't said anything. "Even more exciting," she added, "is the fact that Matthew and Devon have moved into the Penmore Estate!"

I couldn't help it. A small gasp escaped my lips. Someone had renovated the Penmore Estate and I hadn't known about it? After setting all of our stories there, it had always felt as if the Penmore Estate belonged to me and Kitty.

"Furthermore," Mrs. Godfrey continued, "they're being gracious enough to offer tours of the property this Friday at six p.m. to any Whickett Harbor residents who would like to explore this important landmark."

Devon cleared his throat. "Our mother."

Mrs. Godfrey looked confused. "What about your mother, dear?"

"You said *we're* offering the tours." He gestured between himself and Matthew. "But that's our mother's doing. She's hired a small army to get the place ready, and no offense, but the last thing I want is to have the populace tramping through our living space."

I jolted and the egg cracked in my hand. Bright yellow yolk splattered all over my shirt and dripped down my wrist.

Populace? Tramping?

I ground my teeth. If my hand weren't covered in egg yolk, I would've balled it into a fist.

Mrs. Godfrey wasn't dismayed by Devon's attitude, though. She just waved one hand in a dramatic swoop. "So gracious," she repeated. "Teachers will provide extra credit to any students who show proof of attendance. The Penmore Estate is an historic property, and Whickett Harbor is indebted to the Fairfax family for restoring it to its former glory."

She turned to Devon and Matthew. "I'll leave you boys with Miss Bates to sort out your books and cubbies."

As soon as Mrs. Godfrey left, Miss Bates ushered Devon and Matthew forward. "Yes, yes. Books and cubbies. Cubbies and books. So much to—well, we're starting with Culinary Arts today. Making breakfast—always begin with a good breakfast—that's what everyone says, isn't it?" Miss Bates waited for us to laugh, but no one did.

"Well, never mind." Miss Bates ran one hand through her mop of gray hair. She looked perpetually frazzled. "Why don't you jump right in? We're making cheese omelets— that's omelets with cheese. But of course, you knew that. Silly me." She paused. "Have either of you boys ever made an omelet?"

Both of them nodded.

"Our mother hired a personal chef last year so my brother

and I could master the essentials of cooking," Devon said. "She feels it's important for young men to be accomplished in many areas, such as art, culinary skills, a base knowledge of musical theory, and multiple languages."

Miss Bates's mouth hung open. She closed it again after a long moment. "So . . . that's a yes? About the omelets?"

"Yes," Devon repeated. "Matthew and I can make several varieties of frittata."

I could tell Miss Bates had no idea what a frittata was, and I had to admit that I wasn't so sure either. I thought it might be a Mexican dish where you put vegetables and meat into a tortilla.

"Wonderful," Miss Bates said. "Frittata. Yes. That's very—well, you'll have no problem joining in. Pairs though—pairs, as in couples, not fruit. That is to say, we always work together. Devon, why don't you pair up with . . ."

Beside me, Kitty waved madly, squirming like a toddler who had to pee. She was giving Miss Bates her most pleading eyes, but so were a few of the other girls. They giggled, practically knocking one another over trying to get Miss Bates's attention. *Humiliating.* Devon Fairfax had just openly insulted us, and they were still drooling over him as if he were the marshmallow cream inside a whoopie pie. Sure, he was good-looking with his thick dark hair and high cheekbones, but that wasn't enough to make up for his attitude.

At least the boys were less than impressed. Liam Collins told some joke—probably a stupid, sniveling one designed to suck up to Miss Bates—and Nate Crandall coughed the word *loser* into his hand. Then Nate's brother, Ollie, picked his nose and wiped his finger on Liam's pant leg, and all the other boys acted like this was the funniest thing they'd ever seen.

Wonderful. Not that I cared what some rich, snobby boy thought of us. But my face still burned. While I was busy scrutinizing my classmates, Miss Bates's eyes landed on me.

No. I shook my head but Miss Bates just grinned as if she'd made the perfect match.

"Good. Great! Most wonderful. Devon, you can pair up with Jane, and Matthew, why don't you work with Kitty?"

Kitty's fingers dug into my arm. She twirled a lock of spiraled hair around her finger, then exhaled slow as if she were in a yoga class. Beside us, Olivia and Michelle made long drawn-out *oooooooo's* of disappointment. I frowned at Devon. If the other girls wanted him, they could have him.

When he reached me, he stuck out his hand as if he hadn't noticed that mine was covered in raw egg, and then he gave me a condescending smile.

"And you are . . . ?"

I decided to call his bluff. I took his hand and shook,

smearing the egg as much as possible. "Jane," I said. "Jane Sylvia Brannen."

Devon pulled back his hand as if I'd given him a disease, and then he scowled, searching for a towel. Guess he wasn't used to mixing with the populace.

"So, is this your first day of cooking class?" Devon asked.

"It's called Culinary Arts," I corrected, "and no. We had this class last year."

"Oh," Devon said. "I assumed cracking eggs would've been covered on day one, but I suppose it takes some of us longer to master the basics."

"That's right," I said, gritting my teeth and pasting on a fake smile. "Not everyone has a personal chef to teach them Mexican cuisine."

For a moment Devon looked confused, but then he laughed. It was a sharp, bursting laugh. "How cute."

Cute? *Cute?* As if I were one of the elementary kids?

"Well, you're . . ." Words failed me. That never happened. "You're . . . wearing a tie again!"

Devon's cheeks turned crimson. "At least I'm not dressed like a vagabond, as so many others around here."

Secretly, I had to admit that Devon was partly right. People in Whickett Harbor tended to wear old jeans and flannel shirts regardless of the weather. When a holiday rolled around, people put on their *good* flannel shirts. But I wasn't going to admit any such thing to Devon Fairfax.

"Vagabond?" I snapped. "Who says that?"

"Vagabond: someone who—"

"Thank you, Dr. Dictionary. I know what a vagabond is. It may come as a surprise to you, but people in Whickett Harbor know plenty of vocabulary words."

Devon snorted. "I didn't mean to insult you. In fact, I'm thrilled to be someplace less academic for once. It's hard to believe there isn't a private school within a hundred-mile radius for my mother to banish me to, but at least this town won't be full of pathetic wanna-be writers who delude themselves into believing they have talent, then hang all over my mum trying to get her to notice them."

My throat closed up. I thought about my rejection letter from *Girl Power* magazine and swallowed hard. Was I deluded? Pretending I had talent?

"Shall we begin?" Devon asked. He reached out, palm up.

"By all means," I said. I pulled another egg out of the carton and smacked it flat, letting the shell grind into his hand. "It's your turn to crack the eggs."

CHAPTER EIGHT

"Matthew is perfect." Kitty's head was propped dreamily against her hand. "Everything he says is clever. We love all the same books and music. I'm going to be the first girl in grade seven to have an exotic, foreign boyfriend, and we'll date all through high school, get engaged our senior year during the graduation ceremony, and then we'll get married in the summer at Portland Head Light before moving to Wales."

Kitty had her future completely planned out. If only my own future looked half as bright.

Right now, the noise of the lunch room was making my head pound. All the grades ate together at noon and the volume level made the walls vibrate. Sometimes I tried to read at the lunch table, but it was hard to concentrate.

The sixth-, seventh-, and eighth-grade girls ate at one of the long tables at the side of the room, and the boys ate at the table behind ours. The kindergarteners through fifth graders sat up front with the teachers, and the high schoolers had the best tables, along the back wall, farthest away from the lunch line.

"Kitty, you're so lucky you got to meet Matthew first," Olivia said, staring forlornly at the ham sandwich her mother had packed. Olivia had decided to become a vegetarian, but her mother wasn't cooperating. "You sure looked like you were having fun."

"Did I mention that Matthew is perfect?" Kitty said. "He's super funny. And guess what. He loves Hello Kitty too."

"They have Hello Kitty in England?" Jennifer asked.

From the end of the table, Mary Newburg, the Methodist and Episcopal ministers' daughter, lifted her nose out of the book she was reading. "The United Kingdom," she said, "has all of the modern conveniences that we have. In fact, our society descended from theirs, not the other way around."

Mary had been raised by not one but two ministers, so most of what came out of her mouth sounded like a sermon. She loved to point out our faults, and that got old quick.

"Matthew and I couldn't stop talking," Kitty said breathily. "We just had *so* much to say. Matthew knows everything about cooking and traveling, and he wants to be a computer animator someday. Isn't that cool?"

Francie scowled. "You think it's cool that he wants to be another media-driven pawn adding to the meaninglessness of modern society?"

Francie was in ninth grade and was our school rebel, always willing to break the rules. She ate at our table whenever she and the other ninth-grade girl weren't getting along. That day, Joanie was eating with the tenth graders, who sat all mashed together, boys and girls draped over one another.

Was that what our class would be like when we reached tenth grade? For a minute, I imagined what it might feel like to drape myself over a boy. If I was going to write sophisticated, worldly stories, shouldn't I know?

I'd lost the thread of the conversation, but I looked up again when I heard gasps around me. A new girl had emerged from the lunch line, carrying a red plastic tray complete with greasy chicken nuggets and soggy green beans, but somehow she made it appear as if she were walking a runway in Milan. She was tall and stick thin, and she had the exact same shade of hair as Devon. There was no mistaking her features because they looked just like his.

"Oh. My. Goodness," Kitty breathed. "Those shoes are awesome! And I swear I saw those exact pants in a fashion magazine."

I wrinkled my nose. Aside from Kitty, fashionable people

made me grouchy. Their mere presence made me feel short and frumpy.

Matthew waved from the end of his table. "Hey, sis! Want to sit over here?"

The girl's expression shifted as if she'd just stepped in dog poop. "With the little kids? No. Way."

Little kids? That was *my* class she was talking about! My eyes narrowed just as she glanced toward me. She gave me a smile that was half amusement and half smirk before she made her way over to the high school table and settled in between the two best-looking guys in the tenth grade, displacing Joanie with a wiggle and a bump of her curved hips.

Ugh. Another snooty Fairfax? How many of them were there?

Michelle sighed. "She is so pretty." Then she shook her head. "But the person I truly envy is Jane."

My peanut butter sandwich stuck to the roof of my mouth. "Me?"

"Uh-huh. Devon is so good-looking." She paused as if she couldn't quite bring herself to ask, but couldn't bear *not* to. "What's he like?"

"I could listen to his accent all day," Jennifer added.

I didn't point out that after the second egg incident, Devon and I hadn't spoken a word to each other that wasn't directly related to making a cheese omelet. Instead, I thought about what Devon had said about our town.

"I don't care what kind of accent he has," I snapped. "Maybe you all think he's good-looking, but he's not cute enough to tempt me. Devon Fairfax is pompous, he insults other people, and he dresses like a dork."

"Jane!" Kitty said, reaching over to squeeze my hand so hard, it hurt. "Shut up, will you? He's sitting right behind us. He probably heard that!"

I glanced over my shoulder.

"I don't care. He ought to hear me."

Devon *was* directly behind me, but if he'd heard what I said, he didn't show any outward sign. He was busy spreading some sort of soft cheese onto a cracker. There was a thermos beside him and I bet it held something ridiculous like chicken consommé or sparkling water. Crème brûlée?

The other boys were making conversation with Matthew, but Devon was silent. I couldn't help glancing over my shoulder once more, and this time Devon looked right at me.

And he didn't look haughty . . . he looked hurt.

All I wanted was to go home, bury myself under Gram's quilt on the B&B couch, and pretend this day had never happened.

CHAPTER NINE

The school week flew by much too quickly. Mom and Erik drove down the coast so that Erik could see more of Maine, so I had a few days' reprieve, but I knew it wouldn't last. Any day now they'd be back, and this time I'd be expected to spend "quality time" with them.

What would they consider quality time anyway?

My version of quality time was to sit in my kitchen nook writing stories. Usually, I wrote fantasy stories, but this week, I'd written about an obnoxious couple from California who toured Maine only to get lost in a fog that sucked them into another dimension. No one ever saw them again, so the story had a happy ending.

Bitterly, I wondered if this story would be relevant enough for *Girl Power* magazine.

Finally, on Friday afternoon Ana booted me out of the cupboard.

"Okay, Jane. Enough moping. Tonight is the tour of the

Penmore Estate. You've got to be excited about that. The entire town is talking about it. My friend Sarah is on the landscaping crew, and she said the place is incredible."

Ana had on old jeans and a *Life Is Good* T-shirt and her hair was pulled back in a bandanna. She'd been outside working in our garden. Actually, it was her garden because she was the only one who ever worked in it. She wiped away a trickle of sweat and left a smear of dirt along her forehead.

I shook my head. "I'm not going."

"What? Of course you're going! You and Kitty have been daydreaming about that place for years! How many drawings did the two of you do, imagining the inside of the mansion? How many stories have you set there?"

She was right, but I had my pride. If Devon Fairfax was going to look down on tourists at his house, then I wasn't going to be one of them.

"I've changed my mind," I lied. "I don't care what it looks like inside."

Ana shook her head. "You're crazy. I'm dying to see the house." She probably would have argued further, but we heard the rumble of Dad's truck in the driveway. Ana glanced at her phone. "Five forty-five," she muttered. "Not bad."

Dad was notoriously late.

Then I heard a second car pull up. Did that mean Mom and Erik were here?

Ugh.

Ana swatted me on the backside. "Come on, Jane. You can't avoid them forever."

I followed her over and waited while Ana and Dad chatted. Mom and Erik got out of their shiny silver convertible and waved. Who rented a convertible in Maine when it was chilly to downright cold ninety percent of the year?

"Jane! We missed you so much! How are you, sweetie?" Mom flew over to me, making air kisses. Only my mother would give air kisses to her daughter.

"I'm fine," I mumbled.

Ana got into her truck. She was moving faster than usual and I couldn't help feeling as if, despite her directions to me, she was making a speedy getaway. "If you change your mind, maybe I'll see you tonight," she called through the open window as she backed out.

I shook my head. I wouldn't change my mind.

"How was Bar Harbor?" Dad asked, turning to Mom and Erik.

"Wonderful," Erik said. "What a great vista!"

"Wasn't it perfect?" Mom agreed. "I've always loved Bar Harbor."

This was a flat-out lie. Mom couldn't stand Maine. She'd once told me there wasn't an inch of the entire state she could tolerate.

"It would be awesome to film something there," Erik said. "It's getting tough to think of new things to blow up out in California." He laughed uproariously, but I think he was serious.

"Well . . ." Dad said, and then it was obvious he didn't have anything else to say. "There's that."

Mom sashayed over and kissed the top of my head.

"How was your first week of school?"

"Fine."

"Are you still friends with that girl . . . Trixie?"

"Kitty. Mmm-hmm."

"Any cute boys in your grade?" Mom said the words all singsong, and I rolled my eyes, but my mind flashed to Devon. Traitorous mind.

"No."

Mom's smile wavered. "Your father and I met in seventh grade. We were the school sweethearts right up through graduation. Of course, it didn't work out for us in the end, but that doesn't mean—"

"Mom," I groaned. I did *not* want to hear about my parents' failed romance.

Erik rubbed her shoulders. "We're really looking forward to tonight," he said, changing the subject. "A real mansion? Cool, huh? Maybe it's haunted. Ooooo!"

He was doing that thing again where he spoke in an

exaggerated way, as if I were two years old. I glanced at Dad to ask *are you seeing this?* but he avoided my gaze by inspecting a shrub.

Mom had on a bright green dress and stiletto heels, and now she smoothed out the shimmering fabric. It was tight-fitting with a plunging neckline, like something a celebrity would wear on the red carpet.

"So, Jane, are you almost ready to head out? The tours start at six p.m."

"Head out?" I echoed.

"Didn't your father tell you?" Mom glanced at Dad, but he didn't look up. "We're taking you on the tour of the Penmore Estate! We said we'd pick you up at quarter of six."

For a moment, my heart stopped beating. I glared at Dad and he cringed. No, Dad *hadn't* told me because I'd specifi-cally said I didn't want to go. And he could easily guess that I doubly wouldn't want to go with Mom and Erik.

Well, two could play that game.

"Oh, right," I said smoothly. "Dad and I changed our minds. We'll meet you there. He was so excited to go on the tour that I couldn't let him miss out. Right, Dad?"

Dad gave a longing glance at the house. I knew he had a stack of science journals inside that he was dying to read.

"Uh . . ." He paused. "See . . . we thought you could go with—"

Supersonic mind-piercing eye rays of doom.

"Me," Dad finished. He cleared his throat. "Let me just get cleaned up and then I'll take you." He gave Mom a half shrug. "We can all meet there."

My mother's lips pursed tight. Dad headed into the house, his work boots clunking up the front steps. Mom and Erik shuffled awkwardly.

"I'm surprised your father is interested in this kind of thing. There's nothing scientific on the tour that I'm aware of," Mom muttered.

"Actually," I argued, "Dad's interested in many things these days."

Mom snorted. "Like what?"

I tried to think of something non-scientific that Dad was interested in, but everything I came up with tied back to marine biology. Boats? Dad loved his science vessel, *The Clam*. Books? Dad loved books about oceanography. Movies? Dad watched movies with me, but if left to his own accord, he'd choose documentaries every time.

"Women." The word popped out.

"Really?" Erik laughed and Mom's lips parted in surprise. "Your father is dating?"

"Uh-huh."

Okay. It was technically a lie, but once I'd set Dad up with someone, it would be true.

"Wow," Mom breathed.

"That's great," Erik said. "Good for him, right?" He reached over and patted my head as if I were a terrier. "I produced a movie for children once where both of the little boy's parents got remarried to spies who worked for opposing governments. All kinds of explosions in that one."

Finally, Dad came back outside. He'd changed from his old stained blue jeans and T-shirt into a non-stained pair of blue jeans and a less faded T-shirt. I looked down at my favorite baggy overalls with my plain blue shirt underneath. Part of me considered changing, but another part refused to change for the likes of Devon Fairfax.

"Guess we're all ready to head out?" Dad said.

"Sure. We'll follow you over," Erik agreed.

"Are you certain you don't want to ride with us?" Mom pressed, but I just smiled.

"I'm sure."

Mom sighed. "Okay then. See you there."

When we finally left, Dad and I were silent for a long time. I could tell he wanted to say something but couldn't figure out how to get the words from his brain to his mouth.

"You're going to have to spend time with your mother eventually," Dad said at last.

I nodded. "I know. That's why I agreed to go tonight."

"Erik's probably not as bad as he seems on the surface."

"You think? Have you seen his teeth, Dad? They've got to be dentures. They're unnaturally huge and white. And the hair—"

"Jane," Dad warned.

"Fine. I'll give them a chance, but can we at least go the *long* way to the Penmore Estate so I can fortify myself?"

Dad chuckled. "Fortify, eh?" But he turned off on the road that would take us by the sea.

"So how come you're not more excited about this tour? Won't Kitty be there? I thought you'd be champing at the bit to meet this author lady."

I shrugged. "She has an annoying son."

"Oh. Right. The boy from the library fiasco."

I nodded and Dad gave me a sympathetic half-smile. We'd reached the road that paralleled the ocean, so we both stopped talking. The wind was up and the waves were high, crashing against the seawall at every turn. Thousands of water-worn pebbles dotted the pavement where the waves splashed them up and over, making Dad's old flatbed truck rumble and jolt. Most folks avoided this street, but Dad couldn't get enough of the sea. Even when he wasn't at work, he needed to be near it. Needed to hear the bass rumble of the water and feel the sting of salt against his skin.

He rolled down his window and inhaled. Behind us, we could hear the rev of Mom and Erik's rental car, and I bet that Mom was annoyed we'd taken the long way. Dad once told me that the year after I was born, Mom had given him an ultimatum: Move to Hollywood or get a divorce. They'd signed the papers six months later.

He told me that story on days when I was angry that Mom never visited us. Up until now, I'd always had to fly to *her*. And when I did visit, she spent the whole time talking about whatever new guy she was dating. She'd go on and on about how great it was to have me there, but when I got home, she'd forget to call. Or e-mail. Or communicate in any way.

So, Dad's story was supposed to make me blame *him* for not giving in to save their marriage, but I'd never been able to see things that way. The way I saw it, Maine was part of my father, as important as the air in his lungs, and if you loved someone, you'd never ask them to stop breathing, would you? You'd never try to separate them from what they loved most.

Besides, no matter what Dad said, the truth was . . . Mom could've taken me with her if she'd wanted to. According to Kitty, courts always gave custody to the biological mother even if she was wicked. But my mom hadn't wanted me, and

I was grateful for that fact. Leaving me with Dad was the best thing Mom had ever done.

I reached over the seat and grabbed Dad's hand, squeezing it tight. He looked up, surprised, but then I rolled down my window, just like he had, and took a deep breath. The air was so cold it made my nose hairs tingle, but it smelled briny, like seaweed.

Like my dad.

We rode the rest of the way to the Penmore Estate like that, holding hands in the truck cab, covered in a fine layer of ocean mist. When we finally reached the edge of the estate, I hoped the massive front gates might have already closed for the night, but no such luck. We pulled in, then followed the long, winding road up to where the mansion sat. The road was lined with trees, their leaves alternating reds and oranges. Beside the house, a makeshift parking lot had been roped off on the side lawn.

A heavy weight settled in my stomach, and I took several breaths, trying to dispel my dread. If I were Devon, and my house was on display, I'd stay holed up in my room the entire time—especially if I didn't want people there in the first place—so maybe I wouldn't even see him.

Mom and Erik got out of their car and Mom's stiletto heels sunk into the grass. Erik gave her a sympathetic look and I heard him murmur, "Hey, at least this place has class."

I knew Mom felt the same way. This was what she'd always wanted—the high life. Wealth, fame, and all that came with it.

I kept my hand linked with Dad's as we walked up the long cobblestone walkway. Outside, it was dark, but delicate white lights decorated everything: every tree in the yard, the entire outline of the roof, and each of the small balconies that jutted out from the upper-story windows. Dad and I joined the end of a small line of people. While I strained to spot Kitty, he greeted everyone, making the usual small talk.

Just beyond the front door was a line of Fairfaxes, starting with the tall, dark-haired woman in a navy blue business suit who I recognized as J. E. Fairfax. She was followed by Caroline, Devon, and Matthew.

They were all dressed in navy blue, and the boys had blue sport coats with emblems on the front pocket. Their mother clearly had a fixation with dressing her kids alike in the nerdiest clothes known to humankind.

In order to enter the house, people had to shake hands with each of them. The closer we got, the more everything seemed to slow down and become distorted. An imaginary camera zoomed in on tiny imperfections, blowing them out of proportion. I noticed every stained flannel shirt, every person who laughed too loud or shook hands too hard.

The Fairfax family stood with their backs straight, polished and poised. Caroline, especially, seemed to be sneering at everyone as they passed her. She kept leaning over to whisper things to Devon. Were they making jokes? She waved at one of the girls from school, but when she turned back around, she rolled her eyes.

Right then, Devon noticed my presence in the line. He stared at me and it almost seemed as if he'd been about to smile, but I looked away quick. My cheeks burst into flames. If Devon Fairfax stayed in Whickett Harbor, I might need to invest in a personal fire extinguisher for my face. By the time I glanced over again, Devon was busy greeting the people ahead of us in line.

He didn't look at me, and I didn't look at him either, but I could already tell that it was going to be a very long night.

CHAPTER TEN

$\mathcal{D}$espite my mortification, I couldn't help being intrigued. What would a real author's house look like inside? Would the Penmore Estate look anything like the pictures Kitty and I had once drawn in our notebooks?

Sure enough, there was a chandelier, multiple statues, and a huge spiral staircase. I could see two large rooms on each side of the foyer. Small groups were being led on tours by members of the Whickett Harbor Historical Society. I wanted to stare at the grandeur of the place, soaking in the sparkle, but then it was our turn, and Dad reached out to shake J. E. Fairfax's hand.

"Ma'am," he said, inclining his head. "We appreciate your hospitality tonight. I'm Emmett Brannen and this is my daughter, Jane."

Dad and J. E. Fairfax were exactly the same height. Up close, she was really beautiful. Her skin was flawless brown, and she wore the exact amount of makeup to highlight her features. I wondered what Devon's dad looked like, because Devon's skin was very pale. Matthew's too. But Caroline had a lighter skin color than her mother, yet a darker skin color than her brothers, making it appear as if she'd been lying on the beach and gotten the world's most amazing tan. I thought about how pasty my own skin looked in comparison.

"So this is the infamous Jane?" J. E. Fairfax said it with a laugh and a smile as if to assure me that I was off the hook for the trouble Devon and I had caused. She reached over to take my hand, then leaned in as if to tell me a secret. "Jane is my name too. J. E. stands for Jane Elinor. I was named after Jane Austen characters. Jane from *Pride and Prejudice,* and Elinor from *Sense and Sensibility*. But I'm sure you're too young to know much about Jane Austen."

"Actually, I do know about her," I corrected. "My babysitter, Ana, is a big fan. She got me this necklace."

I'd been wearing the necklace every day, and now I opened the book charm so J. E. Fairfax could see inside and read the quote: *Indulge your imagination in every possible flight.*

"How beautiful!"

"We've watched all of the movies based on Jane Austen's books," I added.

J. E. Fairfax's smile dimmed. "Ah. The *movies*. But of course the films don't compare to the novels. In a few years, when you're old enough, you'll be able to read Jane Austen's works for yourself. Has your babysitter read them?"

The answer to that was sort-of. Ana had started reading *Pride and Prejudice,* but then she'd cried because she wasn't a great reader and the language from the 1800s was very different from today. Ana's biggest fear was that she wasn't smart, but she was wrong. She was plenty smart. So, we'd started over again, reading out loud, and we'd figured it out together. It wasn't actually that hard once you got used to it.

"We read *Pride and Prejudice,*" I said.

J. E. Fairfax's eyes shot open and she looked as though she didn't believe me, but Dad jumped in to back me up.

"Jane's a real good reader," Dad said. "She's already read many of the classics—*Wuthering Heights, Great Expectations, Jane Eyre . . .*"

"Oh how wonderful. You must be very proud to have raised such an intelligent daughter."

Dad grinned. "Jane loves to write. She'd like to become—"

I couldn't let him say it. Not in front of Devon.

"Dad, we're holding up the line. Mom and Erik are waiting."

Mrs. Fairfax turned to them and they both gushed over the house and the property, her books and her career. Erik handed her his business card.

"I'm sure the film rights to your books are all taken, but just in case you're ever in need of a director . . . Susan is a screenwriter and I've directed quite a few films."

He was all teeth and gleaming spray-tan, but J. E. Fairfax only had eyes for my dad. She nodded, accepting the card, but she kept glancing over at Dad.

"Thanks for the tour, Mrs. Fairfax," I said, eager to get this over with. I strained on tiptoes to see if I could spot Kitty or Ana in the milling crowd. "We shouldn't keep you any longer."

"Nonsense," J. E. Fairfax said. "It appears you're the very last guests. And it's *Ms.*," she corrected, "not *Mrs.* Not since my recent divorce. But please, call me Elle. I've always gone by my middle name with friends, and there's no need for formality among neighbors, now is there?"

She smiled at my father when she said that part, and Dad smiled back, but I shuffled uncomfortably. Somehow, the idea of the Fairfaxes considering themselves our neighbors felt ludicrous. Sure, they might have a Whickett Harbor address, but otherwise, they lived in another universe.

Ms. Fairfax—Elle—turned toward her kids and made a flourish with one hand. "May I present my children," she said. "Caroline, Devon, and Matthew all go to school with Jane."

I could feel Devon's gaze taking in my windblown hair, sea-spray-soaked jacket, and torn overalls. He kept studying me until I glared at him.

"Such beautiful children," Mom said. "What fun to meet Jane's friends!"

"Mom," I groaned, but Elle had already moved on.

"Tell me, Emmett . . . what do you do for a living?"

Without thinking about it, I locked eyes with my mother and we both made the exact same horror-stricken face. Elle had just given Dad an opening to talk about plankton.

Then I caught myself. I would *not* collude with Mom against Dad.

"I'm a senior research scientist at OSI—that's the Ocean Science Institute," Dad said. "I have a doctorate in planktology, but I combine that with general field research as well. I've just extended our grant to study the effects of ocean acidification on marine plankton to determine how climate change will disrupt the food chain."

Devon's eyes flashed from me to my father. He opened his mouth as if he might be going to say something, but whatever he'd been about to say was eclipsed by his mom's over-the-top reaction.

"Oh, my word! How fascinating! How noble!"

Noble? Dad?

I tugged at his arm. "Dad, we should go if we're going to catch one of the tours."

"Don't be silly," Elle said. "I'm happy to give you a personal tour. After all, I feel like we practically know each other since our children got into mischief together."

Dad blushed. "I don't want to put you to any trouble."

"I wouldn't hear of it! The whole point of this evening is to get to know our neighbors. Isn't that right, kids?"

Caroline gave a small nod, as if she were royalty at court. "Exactly. I think I'll join one of the other groups, so as to meet even more of our new friends."

"Me too," Matthew piped up. I couldn't help noticing that when Matthew left, he joined the group that included Kitty. I waved to her, but she was too busy looking dreamily at Matthew as he approached.

I waited for Devon to make his excuse, but he didn't. He hung back as his mother looped her arm around Dad's elbow.

"So what exactly is plankton?" Elle asked. "They're the little creatures that whales eat, correct?"

Mom and I both rolled our eyes. Then I caught myself. Again.

Dad chuckled. "Plankton is the collective name for organisms that drift with the currents. Of course, there are a few species of plankton that can swim, but not strong enough to avoid being carried along by the tide. Independence isn't their strong suit." Dad laughed like this was some sort of hilarious joke, and Elle laughed as if Dad were actually funny. Which only encouraged him.

"Of course, most people think plankton is one category, but in fact there's phytoplankton, zooplankton, bacterio-plankton . . . or you could divide them into holoplankton or meroplankton based on their life cycle modes."

Someone kill me now.

"There's incredible diversity among plankton since they aren't defined by taxonomy or size. And yet, these tiny creatures provide almost all of the energy for life at sea. They're producers, consumers, and recyclers!"

Dad always thought that statement should induce awe in his listeners. The odd thing was, it did seem to produce awe in Devon. He leaned forward, hanging on every word.

"What's the largest plankton in the ocean?" Devon asked.

"That would be jellyfish," Dad said. "You'd be surprised how large some jellyfish grow."

As Dad talked, we walked around the house. Devon asked Dad one question after another while Elle attempted to interrupt in order to point out some historic feature or a painting they'd had shipped from their home in Wales. The whole time Mom and Erik drooled over everything, and Erik kept mentioning his films with only the slightest tie-ins to the actual conversation.

I was convinced the situation couldn't get any worse, when I heard Dad speak the words I'd dreaded. I'd long since tuned out his impromptu science lecture and I was studying a white marble statue.

"You know, Jane wants to be a writer someday," Dad said. "This is such a wonderful opportunity for her. Not every aspiring author gets to meet someone who's published so many successful books."

Suddenly, plankton didn't seem so bad. I wanted to melt into the floor as Devon turned to me with the king of all smirks.

"You didn't tell me you want to be a writer," he said.

"It's just a hobby," I mumbled, but Mom practically fell over herself contradicting me.

"Jane won a Maine Coast writing contest last year. Best short story in her age group. And she's had two poems published in the *Whickett Harbor Gazette*. She's already submitting her work to magazines. Erik and I are hoping she might spend some time in California with us and learn screenwriting. Wouldn't that be an excellent opportunity, Jane?"

I might have turned around and run—sacrificed the last of my pride for a chance to hide out in Dad's truck until the tour was over—but Elle jumped in. Now she was all over Dad *and* me.

"Good for you!" she said. "That's wonderful, Jane. I love hearing about young people who are serious about writing. Goodness knows my own children want nothing to do with it."

Beside her, Devon kicked at a loose thread on the carpet.

"Maybe you have some advice for Jane?" Erik prompted.

Despite myself, I sucked in a sharp breath of anticipation. Did she? Something other than *write what you know*?

"Of course," Elle gushed. "Jane," she said, very seriously, squeezing my arm, "you must read everything you possibly can. Nothing prepares a writer better than reading."

I let out my breath. *That was it?* I already did that. I tried not to let my disappointment show. "Thanks," I mumbled.

"Come, come," Elle said, "there's one more painting I want to show you all, and then we'll visit my office."

She snaked her arm with Dad's again as she led him toward a huge painting that took up most of the wall in the hallway. I was about to follow, but I stopped to peer over the railing at the scene below, and that's when I heard a familiar laugh.

It was Ana's, coming from the opposite side of the staircase.

A small group had just come out of the dining room, and I saw Ana's blond hair before I noticed anything else. I waved, thinking I'd catch her attention and maybe she'd want to come with us instead. But right then, Dad's laugh made Ana look up. Elle's arm was linked with Dad's, and they were still laughing over something Elle had said. Ana saw them and her eyes seemed to lose their sparkle.

Then I heard Kitty's voice. "Jane! Over here!"

Nobody objected when I made my way down the spiral staircase to the table that was set up with punch and hors d'oeuvres. Kitty and Matthew were standing together, sipping punch, and when I reached them Kitty hopped up and down.

"Did you see them? It's so incredible!" She pointed at my father and Elle. "You needed someone for your dad to date and now look! She's exactly right."

It was true. Elle was everything I'd wanted for him . . . wealthy, sophisticated, with a great house. But she was also related to Devon.

"Jane's dad wants to date my mom?" Matthew said. "Cool. She totally needs to meet someone. She's been depressed since the divorce."

I chewed on my lower lip.

"Of course, you'll have to learn to get along with Devon and Caroline," Kitty mused.

"Trust me," Matthew said, "they're not as bad as they seem. Most of the time, anyway."

"Jane?" Kitty prodded. "Isn't this great?"

Things were moving way too fast. Before I had time to respond, Mom and Erik made their way down the stairs.

"Trixie!" Mom gushed. "It's so good to see you again!"

She'd never met Kitty. Not even once. The only reason Mom knew what she looked like was because I'd shown her pictures.

Mom thrust out her phone. "Would you take a photo of me, Erik, and Jane? I want to get a good one of our whole family so I can have it framed."

Kitty pushed the cell phone back to my mother. "My grandmother won't let me have a phone, so I don't know how to work these," she said coldly.

Mom's face fell, but Matthew jumped in. "I can take it." He gave Kitty an encouraging nod. "It's super easy."

I could tell Kitty was exasperated that he hadn't caught on to her lie, but I didn't blame him. How was Matthew supposed to know my mother's history with family photos? Reluctantly, I stood between her and Erik, posed beneath a glittering chandelier, but the whole time my eyes were focused above.

On Dad and Elle.

CHAPTER ELEVEN

The rest of the weekend couldn't pass quickly enough. On Saturday, Mom and Erik forced me to go hiking with them, but they hadn't checked the weather, so a downpour hit before we were halfway to our destination. Mom kept saying, "This is an adventure. A very fun adventure," even though it was neither fun nor an adventure.

On Sunday we drove to Meryton to see a movie because Erik knew someone who had worked on it, but they hadn't thought to check the rating, and it was rated R. So we ended up seeing an animated squirrel movie instead.

Totally dumb.

By the time school rolled around on Monday, I was glad to have a break. Anything would be better than listening to one more story about how awesome it was on set and how California was the most incredible place in the galaxy.

But when I got to school, Miss Bates had us sit at the lab

tables in the same pairs we'd been in for Culinary Arts so she could make an announcement.

"Good news! So fun! The person seated next to you—that is your partner—together you'll be working on a very special project that you'll be presenting at the Downeast Science Fair. Schools from all around the state—that is to say, our state—will be participating in this event."

A chorus of groans sounded, but Miss Bates ignored them.

"You have two weeks—fourteen days—except if you're only counting school days and then it's not quite so much . . . anyway, what was I saying?" Miss Bates tugged at her cardigan. It was gray and worn with a hole on one side. "Oh yes. You have two weeks to create a project that will educate and excite the public about some aspect of science that is impacting Maine."

"What if we don't know any?" Kenneth asked.

"Pish posh," Miss Bates said. "There are so many to choose from. So many! Decreases in the puffin and moose populations, red tides, jellyfish blooms, erosion, changing sea levels . . ."

"What kind of project?" Mary asked, leaning forward eagerly. "A detailed report? With footnotes?"

That was exactly the type of project Mary loved.

"Oh no," Miss Bates said. "This project is fun! So very

fun! That is to say, you can be as creative as you like." She got a dreamy look on her face that reminded me of how Kitty looked when she talked about Matthew. Miss Bates had never gotten married, but I couldn't help wondering if she'd ever been in love.

"You could create a sculpture, sew a quilt, take photographs, or even—oh yes—write a story." Miss Bates smiled at me. Kitty stuck her hand in the air. "Yes, Kitty?"

"What if I put on a fashion show?"

"Well, that would certainly be unique—most clever, really—but how would that tie into science?"

Kitty thought it over. "Maybe the models could represent scientists?"

Miss Bates scratched her chin. "Possible. Quite possible. But remember, both partners must agree on their project."

I looked over at Devon. What were the chances we would agree on anything?

"I'll give you twenty minutes to discuss your thoughts," Miss Bates said. "That is to say . . ." She seemed to lose her train of thought. "Oh well, bother." She swatted at a fly and then sat down at her desk, leaving us to talk amongst ourselves.

Devon turned to me. "Why don't we choose plankton?" he said, his face glowing with excitement.

I wrinkled my nose. "Plankton?" I repeated. "You've got

to be kidding me. We're not going to convince anyone to get excited about plankton."

"That's not true," Devon said, managing to look as if I'd personally offended him. "Your dad gets excited about it."

"Of course *he* does. It's his job."

"Well, what do *you* want to do?" Devon demanded.

"Why don't we write a story about two people who fall in love as they walk the final stretch of the Appalachian Trail? They can observe our ecology as they travel." I paused. "Maybe I could talk to your mom about how she starts her stories. Do you know if she outlines or just makes up the plot as she goes along?"

Devon's eyes bulged. "That's absurd. No one falls in love while hiking. You're sweaty and smelly the whole time. And the last thing my mother needs is to spend even more time talking about writing."

I'd been trying not to get my hopes up, but now I felt them plummet. If I could talk to J. E. Fairfax one-on-one, then she might tell me the secrets she clearly didn't want to share with just anyone. I'd looked up all of her books online, and not only were they *not* set in Wales, but they were all romances. Now that I knew she was divorced, I was one hundred percent sure she didn't follow her own advice to write what she knew.

"This project is supposed to educate people," Devon argued. "Do you honestly think anyone attending the science fair will stand around long enough to read a whole story? You have to think about your audience. Even I know that."

"Oh really? Well, how about your audience? Trust me, plankton will never be interesting. If you choose that subject, you'll bore everyone to tears."

"Better than some bit of fluff about two people in love."

The fluff comment stung. There was no way he knew about my rejection letter from *Girl Power,* but his lucky barb had landed exactly where he wanted it to—deep under my skin.

I crossed my arms over my chest and for a moment we were both silent.

Devon might have a point. Thinking about your audience *was* important. Maybe I could make copies of the story for people to take home with them? I thought about Dad and the folks he worked with. What kind of plot would be irresistible to someone who loved science? Dad mostly read magazine articles, but when we had a beach day he sometimes brought along a spy thriller.

Hmm. Love and international intrigue as the couple sprinted along the Appalachian Trail with a bad guy chasing them?

"Jane! Are you even listening to me?"

"What?" I'd been chewing on the end of my pen, but now I stopped. "I was thinking about the plot of my story."

Devon stabbed his pencil into his desk so hard, the tip broke off. "Infuriating. That's what you are—infuriating. I'm not going to help you write a romance story!"

"Well, I'm not going to do a whole project on plankton!"

"Fine," Devon said.

"Fine."

All around us the chatter of the other pairs continued, but Devon and I sat in silence, both of us staring at the clock.

"Did you and Matthew decide what you're doing for your project?" I asked Kitty at lunch.

She beamed. "We're going to shoot a music video. Matthew's going to ask his mom if we can have a school dance at the Penmore Estate. Then we'll make tons of posters with science facts on them and film people dancing while holding the posters. Matthew will put the whole thing to music and edit it into a video that can go viral on YouTube. It's not a fashion show, but at least people will be dressed up."

Huh. That was a pretty good idea.

"Do you think Elle will say yes? About holding the dance at Penmore?" I asked.

Kitty scoffed. "Of course she will. Matthew is her son. Besides," Kitty said, "how boring would our video be if we had to shoot it in the school cafeteria?"

I swirled a straw in my milk carton.

"The best part is," Kitty added, "we'll need chaperones."

I looked at her, confused. "Why is that the best part?"

"Because," Kitty said, as if I were clearly being dense, "Ms. Fairfax will obviously be one of them since it'll be at her house, and then your father can be another one. They'll talk, drink punch, and dance together—"

I sucked in a breath. "Kitty," I said, "I don't think Elle Fairfax is the right person for my father to date."

Kitty gave me *the look*. "She's the perfect person, and you know it. She was all over him during the tour of Penmore. And if your mom thinks your father is dating someone as rich and powerful as J. E. Fairfax, she will totally back off. Who knows? She and Erik might even decide to cut their trip short once they see that they're not needed here."

That was a tempting idea. "You think?"

"Well, they flew out to tell you about the engagement, and they've done that. Erik wanted to see Maine. They've done that. And they were worried about you being taken care of. Once they see your dad with Elle Fairfax, they'll know he has prospects."

"Prospects?"

"You know . . . someone else thinks he's desirable, so he might end up as rich and powerful as they are."

"Kitty," I chided, "Dad doesn't care about stuff like that."

"Of course *he* doesn't, but *they* do."

"What about Devon?"

"I knew you'd bring him up," Kitty said, wagging her finger at me. "First of all, Devon is actually a really nice guy. Second, your dad dating Elle would only be temporary. I mean, let's be honest, Jane. We both adore your father, but can you imagine someone like Elle sticking with him long-term? There's only so many times a woman like her could pretend to be fascinated by plankton, even if your father is decently hot for an old guy."

Was that true? I didn't mind *too much* hearing about the things he found exciting. And Dad wasn't that old. He was only thirty-five. Plus, he had lots of other good qualities.

"And," Kitty continued, "even if by some fluke a gorgeous, wealthy, successful woman wanted to be with your dad for more than a fling, wouldn't that be amazing? You'd be related to a best-selling author!"

I let my head fall into my hands. I couldn't get past the

idea of Dad dating *Devon's* mother. I was absolutely certain Devon would hate the idea too. The last thing he'd want was to be connected to me.

"Don't say no, Jane," Kitty begged. "Matthew and I are going to ask Ms. Fairfax today about hosting the dance. Convince your dad to chaperone." She clutched my arm. "Do not let him say he has to work."

"Okay," I said at last. "I guess it can't hurt."

"Invite Ana too," Kitty suggested. "She's always cool to have around."

I nodded. The thought of Ana calmed a little of my anxiety.

Maybe everything would be fine. This visit was all about putting on a show, wasn't it? Mom wanted to show Erik what a great mother she was, Erik wanted to show Mom what a doting fiancé he was, and if Kitty had her way, Dad would show them both that he was just as good as they were.

What could be wrong with that?

CHAPTER TWELVE

On Tuesday, Mom and Erik picked me up after school, and Mom insisted that we try to drive our way out of the gray fog that had saturated the landscape for days, so thick, you could hardly see through it. She was certain that if we went far enough inland, the clouds would eventually break and we'd find a patch of sunlight.

Or a mall. Mom was fine with either outcome.

So we spent that night walking around a mind-numbing box of corporate advertising, with Mom forcing me to try on clothes I'd never wear. She ended up buying me jeans that were too tight, shirts that were too loose, shoes that had heels, and a whole lot of makeup. Blech. The only good thing we bought was my dress for Kitty's music video. We picked a simple black dress because Mom said those were useful for every occasion. I had to admit, Dad never could have managed that task.

Wednesday I begged off, saying I had homework. Very time-consuming homework that would take me all week to complete. But that didn't stop Mom and Erik from showing up Thursday afternoon, right after I'd gotten home from school.

The fog had turned into rain and it was coming down hard, pounding on the roof of the B&B, blowing in gusts against the windows. I was doing my homework at the kitchen island while Ana vacuumed the living room, so I didn't hear the rental car pull up in the driveway.

Mom and Erik let themselves in without knocking. Erik's arms were full of huge plastic bags filled with various-shaped boxes. They stamped their feet to get the wet leaves off their boots and hung up their dripping raincoats by the front door.

"Phew," Erik said. "It's a real deluge out there. Feels almost like a repeat of that hurricane, eh Jane?"

I shrugged just as Ana walked in. She stopped abruptly. Her hair was pulled back in a kerchief while she cleaned, but now she tugged it off and shoved it in her back pocket.

"Susan. Erik. What are you two doing here?"

Mom gave her a fake smile. "Ana dear, I keep telling Emmett . . . Jane doesn't need a babysitter while Erik and I are here. I am, after all, her mother."

"Perhaps," Ana said, "although I will point out that Jane's been home from school for over an hour already."

"Twelve is plenty old enough to be home alone." Mom laughed. "I was on my own at a much younger age."

True, but according to Dad, my grandparents should have been cited for neglect. I didn't think that was a bar anyone should aim for.

Ana's lips tightened into a thin line. "What's in the bags?" she asked, changing the subject.

Erik's eyes lit up. "Ah-ha! I thought you'd never ask. Follow me!"

We walked through both the kitchen and dining room to reach the spacious living room with the fireplace, the daybed sofa, and the antique desks and trunks. Once we were there, Erik dumped out each bag on the braided rug. They were all board games: Hungry Hungry Hippos, Operation, Battleship, checkers, and Pictionary.

"Wow," I said, not sure what else to say.

"I know," Erik said. "Awesome, right? I bought every board game at your local drugstore. And . . . wait for it . . . Susan and I ran into some friends of yours and invited them over. We'll make it a party! Is that awesome, or is that awesome?"

I bristled at the idea that Mom felt as if she could invite people over to *my* house, but I bit my tongue. "Which friends?"

"Trixie," Mom offered. "She was there buying poster board and paint with two boys and a girl. Violet is going to drop them off shortly."

Two boys and a girl? Could she mean Matthew, Devon, and Caroline? Kitty had told me that Caroline wanted to help plan the dance, but why would Devon be with them?

"All right," Erik said, clapping his hands together. "Let's get this board game extravaganza set up."

"Actually Erik," Ana offered, "I think we could probably skip Operation . . . and the hippo game. The kids are twelve, you know?"

She was being really nice, but Erik looked crushed. "Really? I love Operation. But you're the expert. Only, the hippos have got to stay. You're never too old for hippos, am I right, Jane?"

I smiled weakly, but when Erik went out of the room to drag in one of the small tables from the dining room, Ana lifted her eyebrows and bugged out her eyes at me, so I couldn't help but laugh.

"Hey! Who else is Unit A? We're on tables. Unit B covers snacks."

"I'll help with tables," Mom said, although she didn't sound very happy about it.

"Guess we're on snacks," Ana said. We went into the kitchen and rifled through the cupboards. There was an old box of cheese crackers. A couple apples that weren't entirely shriveled. Then I heard the slow rumble of Granny V's minivan pulling into the driveway.

I watched them all pile out, and as I'd suspected, it was Devon, Matthew, and Caroline who slid out of the back seat. They ducked under their jackets as they ran to the front door, and I had just enough time to glance around my kitchen, taking in the piles of dirty dishes, science magazines, and sample jars.

Ana let them in and got a wet hug from Granny V. Mom and Erik came in from the other room and Erik did this stupid, raised-hands, pulsing dance while singing, "Let's get this party started."

Mortifying.

Matthew grinned and danced along, but Devon and Caroline just stood there frowning.

"I bought some snacks for you kids," Granny V said, handing Ana two bags full of chips, cookies, M&M's, and bottles of ginger ale. "Shall I come get them before or after dinner?"

"Before dinner would be good," Ana said. "Thanks for the snacks, Violet. You know how bare Emmett's cupboards are."

Granny V winked. "Wouldn't want them snacking on sea

kelp, now would we?" She waved to the rest of us. "Have fun!"

I watched as the others filtered into my house. Matthew and Kitty were talking to Mom and Erik, and Caroline kept drawing back in horror at various things of my dad's, like the complete fish skeleton mounted on the wall, the preserved puffer fish, the empty crab and lobster shells, or the framed photo of a comb jelly, which was Dad's favorite species of plankton.

"Good god," she breathed, shivering as if she'd seen something awful. She hurried to catch up to Kitty and Matthew. That left only Devon.

"So, this is where you live?" He glanced around the packed room.

"Yup."

He picked up a jar. "Why doesn't your father store these at his lab?"

"He does, mostly," I said. "But sampling is kind of a compulsion for him. He can't help himself, so wherever we go . . ." I indicated the jars and the large cooler beside our refrigerator designated for overflow.

"Is that a comb jelly?" Devon asked, pointing toward the photo.

I couldn't hide my surprise. "Yeah. It is."

"Cool. Jellyfish are amazing."

"My father would agree with you."

"What about you?" Devon asked. "Would you agree?"

I paused. "Actually, I would. Dad says comb jellies are one of the oldest species on Earth. Five hundred million years old. When I see them, it's like looking back in time."

Devon grinned. He looked as if he could spend all day in my dining room, but I nudged him forward. We joined the rest of the group just as Caroline gushed to my mother, "I know! I hate this place too. It's so . . . filthy. If I were Jane I'd totally want to move to California."

My body stiffened. Why were they talking about me moving to California? And my house *wasn't* filthy; Ana had just vacuumed. Or had Caroline meant that Whickett Harbor was filthy? Either way she was wrong.

Before I could say anything Kitty rushed over.

"Jane . . . Guess what! I have incredible news. Ms. Fairfax said yes! We're going to have a dance at Penmore! Can you believe it? We can shoot the video first and then we'll have the rest of the night to party."

"That's awesome."

"A music video?" Erik said. "On location at the Penmore Estate? Brilliant!"

"I know," Matthew agreed. "Isn't it cool? We're going to invite everyone at school from sixth to twelfth grade. Mum said we can have the dance next weekend, but that only gives us a week to prepare."

"You'll need cameras, lights, and editing software," Erik said. "A moving dolly would be great. There will have to be a sound system, and a script, of course."

Kitty paused. "Uh . . . we thought we'd just have everyone get together and dance while holding some posters. Then we'd film it on Matthew's phone."

Erik laughed. He patted them both on their heads and said, "Aww. That's adorable. But we can do much better than that. If you'd like some help, I've directed a few music videos in my time. One or two of them have even won a Grammy."

"Wow," Matthew said. "That would be incredible. You'd really help us?"

Erik preened. "Of course. Now, my young protégés, come over here and I will tell you how it's done. Ana, you should come too." He motioned her over with a dramatic wave of his hand. "You," he said, "could be our star."

Ana looked mortified, but she took her place with Erik, Kitty, and Matthew around one of the tables. The games were forgotten. In another corner, Mom and Caroline were deep in conversation about god-only-knew-what, and that left me and Devon standing awkwardly beside a bag of chips.

"Battleship?" Devon asked.

I shrugged. It was better than standing around doing nothing.

We sat down on opposite sides and set up our ships. I waited for him to say something, but conversation wasn't Devon's strong suit. Eventually, we began calling out numbers, but I couldn't tell who was winning.

"So, will you be in your brother's music video?" I asked when the silence had dragged on too long.

Devon shook his head. "No. I don't dance."

"What?" I asked, feigning shock. "You mean your mother didn't pay for you to have private dance lessons?"

"Of course she did," Devon said. "I didn't say I can't dance. Any idiot can dance. I said I *don't* dance. There's a difference."

I rolled my eyes. "I have never met anyone as arrogant as you."

"Arrogant?" Devon said. "Hardly. I'm merely stating a fact."

"Yes, but you're stating it in such a way that implies you're better than the rest of the . . ." What was the word he had used? ". . . populace."

"A fact is just a fact," Devon said. "I didn't state it in any way at all. If you understood it as a slight against Whickett

Harbor, then perhaps you ought to ask yourself which one of us is truly embarrassed by this place."

Argh! The nerve of him!

I'd had enough. I stood up, reached over the partition, and grabbed his nearest battleship.

"There," I said, pulling it off the board and dumping it unceremoniously in his lap. "I sunk your battleship. Game over."

As I walked away I heard Devon mutter, "On top of everything, she cheats."

I headed toward the kitchen, but Kitty called to me. "Jane, we need your help. We have to find a good environmental cause for our music video."

"It needs to be colorful," Erik added. "Vibrant and hip."

A vibrant, hip environmental problem? I wrinkled my nose. "Uh . . . how about butterflies? Maine is part of the monarch butterfly's migration route, but they might end up on the endangered species list. Biologists are asking people to plant milkweed gardens to help them out."

"That sounds good," Matthew said. "Everyone loves butterflies."

"There's also bees," I added. "If the bees die, they won't be around to pollinate, so there would be no fruits and vegetables. In some parts of China, farmers already have to pollinate flowering trees by hand. I saw pictures online. But if we stop using pesticides and more people become bee-keepers, we could support the bee population. Some people are even beekeeping on rooftops in cities."

"Wow," Kitty said. "Really?"

"Don't forget lobsters," Ana added. "Maine's coastal economy depends on lobsters, but as the ocean gets warmer, they're not able to grow their shells properly, so they have to migrate to colder water. The southern New England lobster-men are almost out of business already, and someday Maine lobstermen, like my dad, might be too."

"Huh." Erik sat back in his chair. "Susan and I just had lobster rolls yesterday. They were cheap."

"Sure," Ana said, "that's because we've got a glut due to all of the southern lobsters moving north, but it won't last."

"There's nothing more iconic than the Maine lobster," Erik said. "What do you say, kids? Lobsters, bees, or butterflies?"

I would have chosen lobsters, hands-down, but that's when my mother piped up from across the room.

"Go with the butterflies," she said. "There's nothing sexy about lobsters."

What? Had my mother really just said that?

"Sexy?" Kitty asked, scrunching up her nose.

Mom shrugged. "You're making a music video. No one wants to watch a bunch of kids dressed in lobster costumes wiggling their nonexistent hips."

"Butterflies don't have hips either," I said, but Caroline took up Mom's argument.

"But they do have wings. Gorgeous, colorful wings that would look incredible waving around as people danced."

Kitty looked at Matthew and then she gave me an apologetic half shrug. "Butterflies are really pretty. We could call it the Butterfly Ball."

I couldn't believe they'd just chosen their environmental cause based on what was better looking. Mom and Caroline joined Kitty, Matthew, Ana, and Erik and soon they were in the thick of planning the ball. I closed my eyes and tried not to scream.

That's when Devon came over to stand beside me.

"I can't believe they just chose their environmental cause based on what looks best."

"I know!" I said, before I could stop myself. "Dad says people are swayed by charismatic mega-fauna."

"What the heck?" Devon laughed.

I had to admit, it sounded funny. "Well, *charismatic* means that something attracts attention. *Mega* means big, and *fauna* means animals, so he means that people are more apt to help save something that's big and cute, like a polar bear, than they are to care about the creatures we can't see, like plankton, even though plankton are the base of the food chain and they create half of the world's oxygen."

"Wow," Devon said. "You know a lot about this stuff."

I shrugged. "You don't grow up with my dad and not know about science. Especially the virtues of plankton."

"So maybe you should write what you know?" Devon said.

"Excuse me?"

Devon sighed. "I'm just saying . . . if you wrote an article and I took photos, we could educate people about something that's really important."

I took in a deep breath. We did need a project. And the idea of choosing something that would normally get overlooked was appealing.

"All right," I said at last. "You win."

Devon's eyes widened. "This might be the first thing we've ever agreed on."

"Don't let it go to your head," I warned him.

"Trust me," he said. "I won't."

CHAPTER THIRTEEN

"So, Dad . . . what would you say to taking me and Devon out on *The Clam* this weekend?"

Dad looked up from his computer where he was carefully charting ocean temperatures. His glasses had slipped down the bridge of his nose, and he looked at me over the top of them. "You kids want to go out on the boat?"

"Yeah," I said. "Remember that science project I told you about?"

"Sure." Dad nodded. "You're writing a story, right? Love and adventure on the Appalachian Trail?"

"Actually," I said, "I'm not. We have to work with a partner, and my partner is Devon."

"Ah. And Devon doesn't want to help you write a romantic adventure story?" Dad's voice was full of sympathy.

I shook my head. "We've decided to choose plankton instead."

There was a moment of stunned silence while my father stared in my direction. "Plankton?" he said at last, blinking rapidly. "That's what you chose?"

"Yup."

I waited for the burst of jubilation, but it didn't come.

"Are you just doing this for me?" Dad swallowed hard. "Because I want you to choose something you really care about."

I set one hand on Dad's arm. His skin was rough from all the time he spent outside on the water. "I do care about plankton. I mean, yeah, sometimes I get tired of hearing about it, but mostly it's pretty cool."

A grin spread slowly across Dad's face. I couldn't remember the last time I'd seen him smile so wide.

"Of course I'll take you on the boat. I can teach you how to do some sampling and then we can go back to the lab and use the microscopes." Dad shut his computer off. "When do you want to go?"

"I don't know. Devon said he was free all day on Saturday." I paused, and then before I'd had time to think it through, I blurted out, "Maybe you should invite Elle too."

Dad's forehead crinkled. "You think she'd want to join us?"

It was hard to imagine Elle Fairfax on Dad's science vessel, but it was too late to take my words back now.

"Sure. I bet she'd jump at the chance to get out on the water."

Dad looked pleased. "Okay then. I'll invite the whole family."

I cringed. Did I really want the entire Fairfax family on our boat trip?

The answer to that was, decidedly, no.

Saturday morning I sat at the kitchen table eating dry cereal because we were out of milk. The weather was windy, but there wasn't any rain, so we were definitely going out on the boat. Kitty had come to my rescue and invited Matthew and Caroline to her place to plan the Butterfly Ball, so it would be just me, Devon, my father, and Elle.

"This is perfect," Kitty had said. "It'll be almost like your dad and Elle are on a date."

Was that what I wanted? Why had I even suggested that we ask her?

A sharp rapping sound gave me a jolt. Erik's face pressed up against the windowpane, and he waved when he saw me.

"Hey, kiddo!" His voice was muffled through the glass. Could I pretend I hadn't seen him? Probably not. I slid off the stool and opened the front door.

"Good morning!" Erik was far too cheerful for eight a.m.

Beside him, Mom stood with her arms crossed over her chest looking as though she'd rather be anywhere else, but when she saw me her face relaxed.

"Morning, Jane. You're up and dressed early."

"So are you." I paused. "What are you guys doing here?"

"Erik thinks we should take one of those lobster boat charter trips," Mom said. "There's one that goes out at eleven. We wondered if you were free."

A lobster tour? I couldn't help it—I laughed out loud. No self-respecting Maine native would go on one of those. They were strictly for tourists.

"What's wrong with a lobster trip?" Erik asked. "We could catch us some dinner. You like lobster, right Jane?" He did this thing where he gave me a mock one-two punch. "Actually, I take that back. Who doesn't like lobster, am I right? So what would be better than catching our own?"

"Well"—I chewed my lower lip—"it's just that paying a lot of money to watch a lobsterman do his job would be like paying to ride in a delivery vehicle. It's just . . . ordinary."

"For you, maybe," Erik said, looking perplexed.

Mom fixed him with a hard stare. "See? I told you."

Dad and Ana had been upstairs, but now they wandered into the kitchen. Dad's jawline was stubbly and he still seemed half awake. Ana looked surprised to see Mom and

Erik, but she didn't comment, just went straight to the cof-
feepot. Mom's eyes darted between the two of them.

"This is a late start to the day for you, Emmett. No samples to collect at dawn?"

"Actually, I'm taking the boat out in a few hours," Dad
said. "I'm bringing Jane and a friend of hers out today so
they can do some sampling for their science project."

Erik's eyebrows shot up. "That's great! Maybe we could
save a bundle and go out on *your* boat. That would be very
cool. Actual science in progress."

We all stared at Erik, but he just kept on grinning. He
was wearing a blue shirt with pineapples on it, bright white
shorts, and yellow-and-black shiny flip-flops. His hair had
been combed through with so much gel that I doubted a
strong gale could have moved it.

Mom cringed. "Erik, honey, trust me. Going out on
Emmett's boat is the last thing anyone would want to do."

Across the kitchen, Ana's eyes flared. She'd just taken
a mug out of the cupboard, but now she plunked it on the
counter with a bang. "Excuse me, Susan, but just because
you don't enjoy something doesn't mean no one else will."

"Oh really?" Mom said. "So, are you going on this trip?"

Ana hesitated, but Dad intervened. "Sure she will." He
turned to Ana. "Come with us, Ana. We'd love to have

you. Maybe you could drive the boat while I'm teaching the kids?"

"I don't know." Ana filled a measuring cup with water and poured it into our old-fashioned machine. There was a loud noise as the coffee started to percolate, and then the rich smell filled the kitchen.

"Anyone else coming?" Erik asked.

"J. E. Fairfax," I said. "Elle, I mean."

"You invited J. E. Fairfax on your science vessel?" Mom repeated, staring at Dad. "And she said *yes*?"

The opportunity to rub Mom's nose in this was too much to resist. "Yup," I said. "She likes Dad a lot, if you must know."

Some people think it's a cliché to say that someone's jaw dropped open in surprise, but in Mom's case it was the literal truth.

Dad blushed. "That's not true," he said. "She's just coming along for the boat ride."

Ana took a gulp of her hot coffee and then winced. "You know," she said, "I think I would like to go out on *The Clam* today. It's been a while."

"We'll join in too," Erik said, "if we're invited." He nudged Mom in the ribs. "Come on, babe. You want to spend time with Jane, and I want to get out on the water again. This is ideal. Besides, I'd love to talk to that J. E. Fairfax woman some more. I really think we could do some edgy adaptations of her books, you know? Reconceptualize the franchise."

Since J. E. Fairfax wrote romance novels, it was hard to imagine that they needed any explosions added to them, but I bit my tongue. I could tell that Mom was going to do the objecting for me.

"Erik," Mom whined, "this is a genuinely bad idea. The wind is strong today, which means high waves."

"What? You don't think I've got my sea legs?" Erik said. "Nah. It'll be great. We're all going to spend quality time together. What could go wrong?" He helped himself to a mug from the cupboard and handed it to Ana. "Would you get me some of that coffee?"

"Sure." Ana poured him a steaming cup.

"You're a gem," Erik said. "Diamond in the rough. You ever want to be in the movies, you know where to find me." He winked.

Mom scowled. Ana gave me and Dad another bug-eyed look. Dad frowned. In fact, right now no one looked happy.

Erik dug around in our refrigerator for creamer. "Emmett, what time are we heading out?"

Dad looked trapped. "Uh . . . noon?"

"Perfect." Erik clapped his hands together. "Okay, people. This is going to be great. Now, who's up for a big breakfast? Emmett, you got eggs and bacon? Ana, you a fan of hollandaise sauce? Jane . . ." He gave me that tilted-head look that reminded me of a car salesman on TV. "I know you don't want boring old cereal when we can have the biggest, downeast breakfast known to human kind." He snapped his fingers. "Blueberry pancakes. We absolutely need blueberry pancakes with real maple syrup. And applewood sausages. Ahhh, this is going to be incredible."

"Incredible," Dad mouthed, making me laugh. Mom saw him, and the corner of her mouth twitched up. She shook her head fondly, but no one made a move to stop Erik from rifling through our cabinets. No one made a move to help, either.

"Come on, people," Erik said. "This is vacationland. Time spent in Maine is never wasted. This is the way life should be."

That was every Maine slogan ever invented.

"Girls, you're unit one. Go out there and pick us some wild blueberries, gather sap from the pine trees, harvest some oats. Emmett, you and me are unit two and we're on the eggs, bacon, and hollandaise sauce. Let's go, people. This light's not going to last forever."

I followed Mom and Ana out the door. "I am *not* picking blueberries," Mom said. "We'll drive to Safeway. We can get pancake mix there as well."

"And milk," I added. "And uh, eggs, bacon, and hollandaise sauce."

"Ayuh," Ana agreed, rolling her eyes. "There's already a jug of maple syrup in the cupboard." She paused, studying my mom. "So, is Erik always like this?"

Mom gave an exaggerated sigh. "God help me. He is." She looked at me. "But if you give him a chance, he grows on you. I promise."

Over the years, Mom had made a hundred promises that she'd never kept. Promises to show up in Whickett Harbor for my birthday. Promises to take me to Australia when she'd struck it rich. Promises to do better about remembering to call me every week. I'd long ago learned to be skeptical whenever I heard those two words come out of Mom's mouth.

But this time, I suspected she might be right. Hard as I was working to hate Erik, it was already more difficult than it had been when they'd arrived. He was like an overgrown kid, the way he got excited about stuff like game day, or helping out with the music video, or making the best breakfast.

Of course, Mom had to go and ruin my fond feelings.

"Erik has totally fallen in love with Maine," she said. "He keeps joking that we should move back here." She laughed. "Can you *imagine*?"

Ana and I exchanged glances. Yes, we could imagine, seeing as we lived here.

I sunk low in my seat, all traces of warmth banished completely.

CHAPTER FOURTEEN

Three hours later, our bellies were full with what I had to admit was the best breakfast I'd ever eaten. Fluffy blueberry pancakes with maple syrup, smoky sausages, eggs Benedict, extra thick bacon, and fresh-squeezed orange juice. Erik did most of the actual cooking, but everyone pitched in.

By the time we all left the house, Mom and Ana were chatting about which celebrities Mom had met, and Dad and Erik were talking about why epic movies set on the ocean were filmed in studio water tanks instead of on location. It almost seemed a shame when we split up into our separate vehicles.

I rode with Dad and Ana, and as we arrived at the dock I saw Devon standing by the boat fiddling with the lens cap of a fancy camera. Elle waved when she saw us. Even in casual clothes, she still looked glamorous, and I couldn't help the small surge of wonder that spread through me. How was it possible that a famous author was going out on my father's boat?

"Afternoon," Dad greeted them when we'd all piled out. He paused and I noticed him glance at Elle's shoes. Her *high-heeled* shoes. No one wore heels on a boat. "So," he said, "have you two spent much time at sea?"

Elle shook her head. "No. We aren't exactly seafarers, but today we're being bold."

"Isn't most of Wales coastal?" I asked.

Devon looked up, and Elle seemed impressed. "Why yes, but we're from the area inland near the border."

"Plus, my father always got seasick," Devon offered. "So he preferred to holiday in the Lake District."

"Well, I'm happy to have you on board," Dad said. "You two remember Susan, Erik, and Ana?"

Devon and Elle nodded. "Of course. So nice to see you all again." Elle glanced at Ana. "I didn't realize you were a friend of Emmett and Jane."

"Ana is more than a friend," Dad said. "She's . . ."

"Family," I filled in for him.

"Oh," Elle said. "How lovely."

Dad jumped on board the boat, and then he tossed life jackets to everyone waiting on the dock. Including me.

"Dad," I groaned. "I've been out on *The Clam* hundreds of times, *and* I know how to swim."

My father shook his head. "You know the rules, sprite."

I sighed, fastening the bulky vest around my chest with a click. *The Clam* was an old lobster boat that Dad had gotten used when Buzz Jackson retired. There was a cabin in the front of the boat and a flat back where Dad kept his equipment. It was a good size for a lobster boat, but it wasn't exactly set up for a pleasure cruise. There weren't any chairs, but there were huge coolers where Dad kept his samples once he'd gathered them. One by one, Dad helped each person step from the dock onto the boat.

Devon had a huge grin on his face when he hopped onto *The Clam*.

Elle tripped gracefully into my father's arms as she boarded, and I wondered if she'd done that on purpose.

A few minutes later, the rumble of the boat's engine made the whole thing come alive. I could feel the low thrum up my legs, radiating through my entire body. That sound was pure anticipation. I sniffed the air, thinking about how I'd describe the smell if I were writing a scene on a boat. Diesel and seaweed—usually rotting seaweed because inevitably some piece of green muck got stuck somewhere until it baked in the hot sun. It wasn't a smell everyone loved, and I could see my mother and Elle scrunching up their noses. They each sat on a separate cooler, both with one leg crossed over their knee.

It struck me then how much they looked alike with their long dark hair and tall elegance. Even the way they held themselves was similar. Was it the tilt of the chin? Or something in the eyes?

Ana, on the other hand, was nearly a foot shorter, and her blond hair glinted in the sunlight. She wore sturdy sneakers that had scuff marks and a hole in the toe, but the rubber soles would keep her steady as the boat shifted on the waves. She cast off the fenders as Dad manned the wheel and I stowed the lines, the three of us working like a well-oiled team.

Devon hovered next to me, snapping pictures.

"Here." I threw him one of the ropes. "Make yourself useful. You can hank the bow line."

"Hank?"

"It means coil them and then wrap a piece of the rope around the coil. Like so." I showed him how I'd done the stern line so he could copy me. "Dad has a locker in the cab where we can stow them along with the fenders."

"What are fenders?" Devon asked.

"They're bumpers that prevent the boat from crashing against the dock."

Devon took care of his line, then wandered over to where Ana was checking the equipment. "How do you guys know how to do all this stuff?"

Ana laughed. "My father is a lobsterman, so he had me working on his boat as soon as I was old enough to tug in a trap. It's second nature by now." She nodded at me. "It's the same for Jane. She's been going out on expeditions with her dad since she was three years old."

"Wow." Devon picked up his camera and snapped a bunch of photos, but I pretended not to notice.

Dad idled the boat into the open ocean, then finally kicked the engine into higher gear once we'd passed the final marker. I felt the familiar lurch and the rush of the wind against my face. No matter how hot it is on shore, once you're on the ocean and the spray hits your skin, you feel chilly. *The Clam's* wake made white, foamy streaks behind us.

The sea *was* choppy, but the boat easily rode each crest and dip. I could tell that Mom and Elle were freezing, because they hugged their knees to their chest, but Devon looked happier than I'd ever seen him, standing in the stern, looking out at the open sea.

I ducked into the cab and a few minutes later, Devon followed.

"Where are you taking us?"

On the map, Dad pointed just north of the string of small islands dotting the coastline. "You kids are going to help me do some sampling today," he said. "I'm working on a project measuring the effect of climate change on plankton in the Gulf of Maine."

"Cool," Devon breathed.

Dad pointed to two large sets of lines on the chart. "See this? That's the Labrador Current, which brings in cold water from the arctic. And this one is the Gulf Stream. It's the most important current in our hemisphere." His rough finger traced a path. "The Gulf Stream starts in the Gulf of Mexico, stretches around Florida, moves up the East Coast, and then it goes all the way to Europe in a complex, swift loop. Both of these currents meet in the oceans off Maine's coast and when warm and cold water combine, they create the perfect conditions for plankton."

"That's good, right?" Devon asked.

"Definitely. Plankton are the base of the food chain, so every other form of life in the ocean depends on them. The problem is, as the oceans get warmer, the Gulf Stream is slowing down, so we're monitoring this stretch of water to keep track of what's happening."

"What if it slows down too much?" I asked. "That would harm the Earth, right?"

Dad laughed. "Sprite, the Earth is stronger and more resilient than you can imagine. The problem isn't whether things like this will harm the planet, it's whether they will harm *us*."

"Really?" Devon leaned forward.

"Yup," Dad said. "Life on Earth won't disappear if our climate heats up, but certain species will thrive while others die out, and we'd rather not be one of the species that dies out. But that's certainly not a guarantee. Some human species have already come and gone; like Neanderthals. We have to remember that life on this planet existed for millions of years before us, and there's a good chance it will exist for millions of years after us."

"Which species would thrive if the climate gets warmer?" Devon asked.

Dad rubbed his chin. "Lots of them. Toxic algae blooms, mosquitos, ticks, snakes, sharks . . . jellyfish."

I thought about a planet teeming with the kinds of life that humans couldn't tolerate. Maybe instead of bumper stickers saying SAVE THE EARTH, we needed bumper stickers that said SAVE THE HUMANS.

Dad chuckled. "Don't look so dire, Jane. If we play our cards right, we might be able to earn ourselves a bit more time on the cosmic scale. You know that's why I work so hard, right? I'm working for you—so you and your kids can inherit a world as beautiful as the one I've lived in."

Huh. That was why Dad worked so hard? I'd always assumed ocean science was Dad's version of my writing.

Something he just loved to do. It had never occurred to me that maybe I was part of why Dad put in such long hours.

I wanted to say something, but I didn't get a chance because Ana came up beside Dad and let out a huge sigh. "Erik and Elle are feeling a little queasy already."

Dad frowned. "That'll only get worse when we slow down to throw out the plankton nets."

"I know," Ana said. "It's a bit late, but I don't suppose you've got any Dramamine on board? Peppermints, maybe?"

Dad shook his head. Why would he? None of us got seasick. Now that I stopped to think about it, the waves were pretty high today. The boat rose and fell, and spray soaked every inch of the bow. A minute later, Mom stomped into the cab.

"Emmett, it's far too rough to be out today."

"It's not that bad," I argued. "Dad and I have been out in weather way worse than this."

"Oh, you have?" Mom said, hands on her hips. She glared at Dad.

"Susan, we're fine and you know it," Dad argued. "We'll be where we need to be in a few more minutes and then it won't take long to let the kids draw a few samples. It's not my fault the sea is rough today."

Mom snorted. "Nothing's ever your fault, is it?" She

turned and stomped back the way she'd come. Dad and Ana exchanged looks, and I saw Elle watching them.

I left the cab and stared out at the vast ocean. The swells didn't feel threatening to me, but maybe they should. According to Dad, the sea wouldn't care if it swallowed us up. We were just a little blip in space and time.

Devon joined me, and we were both quiet for a long time. I wondered if he was thinking the same things I was, about how old the planet is and how young we were in comparison.

Just then, a whale spouted in the distance. Devon gasped and we both watched as its slick back crested the surface. Even from far away it was huge. Devon lifted his camera as if he might snap a photo, but then he set it down again. "That was amazing," he breathed.

I nodded. Yes. It really, truly was.

CHAPTER FIFTEEN

$\mathscr{E}$ventually, Dad slowed the boat and Ana took over at the wheel. Elle sat huddled against the stern with Erik next to her, explaining how a chase scene could pick up the pace of her novels.

"A little pizzazz would take your franchise into a whole new stratosphere. Big money," Erik said. "It's what people want." He used his hands to create an imaginary marquee. "Big. Bold. Edgy. The world at stake."

Was that really what people wanted? Jane Austen didn't have any explosions in her books, and they'd been popular for hundreds of years. I didn't argue, though. My attention was distracted by my mother, who stood with her arms folded, glaring out at the dark green sea as if it were her mortal enemy.

"Jane?" Dad said. "Are you paying attention?"

Dad knelt beside a pile of equipment as Devon took photos of each item.

"Okay. Here's how we take samples . . . We're going to attach this jar onto our plankton net, like so." Dad screwed a long jar onto the end of a large triangular net. The net was designed with a jar attachment at the bottom. "See these filters along the top of the jar? They'll allow water to flow out, but they'll keep the plankton in."

Dad handed Devon a clipboard and pen. "You'll need to keep track of our GPS coordinates, time, date, temperature, weather conditions . . . Most importantly, you'll need to write down how deep we're going to drop our nets."

My father picked up the net and line. "Look here. The nets are weighted to allow them to sink. We'll measure out a certain length of line depending on how far down we want the net to go. We'll also keep track of how fast the boat is moving and how far we drag the netting. That way, when we get back to the lab and the machines determine how many organisms are in each sample, we'll know how much water we filtered. Understand?"

Devon's face stretched into a huge grin. "Yeah. It's math."

My father laughed. "That's right. Math, not magic. Science is much more concrete than most people think. We take a measurement. Chart it. Repeat. Then we watch to see if there's a trend."

"But won't your results be different every day?" I asked.

Dad nodded. "Of course. Nature is always changing.

That's why we're not as interested in day-to-day numbers as we are in the rate of change—that means how fast or slow changes are happening and what direction they're taking. We're less concerned about a week or a month's worth of data. Instead, we look at five years or ten years . . . sometimes even more. The time series for the sampling we're doing today is ten years."

Devon and I both gasped. "You've been working on this for ten years?" That meant he'd started when I was two years old. The same year Mom had left.

"That's right," Dad said. "I'm just one of several scientists responsible for these measurements, but they're important because so many species depend on plankton."

"Like whales?" Devon asked.

"Yes. Whales are one," Dad said. "There's a species called the right whale that's on the verge of extinction. There are only about four hundred of them left. They come to Maine to feast on the plankton where it ought to be most abundant, but as the ocean warms up, the plankton are no longer thriving, so their food source isn't here.

"But humans are another species that depends on plankton," Dad said. "Not only do we eat the fish that eat the plankton, but we also need them to take carbon dioxide out of the air. Did you know that plankton remove more carbon dioxide from our atmosphere than trees do?"

I frowned. "Really?"

"Yup," Dad said. He held out his hand with his palm cupped as if he were holding an imaginary rock. "Think about a lump of coal. Now imagine that lump of coal getting thrown into a fire. After a while, it's gone, right? Where did it go?"

"It changed form," Devon said. "Into a gas."

"Exactly." Dad nodded. "Just because we can no longer see something doesn't mean it isn't still there. Now, imagine the Earth as a battery and the sun is our power source. Photosynthesis is the way plants turn the sun's light into the battery's energy.

"Phytoplankton—that's the kind of plankton that's made up of plants—absorb the sun's energy through photosynthesis, and when these tiny plants die, they sink down to the bottom of the ocean. After millions of years, buried under a lot of pressure, they become what we call fossil fuels . . . like coal and oil. Everywhere we find fossil fuels, it's because that piece of land was once covered by an ocean."

"Fossil fuels were once *alive*?" Devon said.

"Yup. It took millions of years to create them, but guess when their energy gets released."

"When we use them?"

"Exactly. So . . ." Dad stuck out both hands palms up as if he were measuring two objects. "Millions of years to store the energy . . . but less than a hundred years to release it. As all that carbon dioxide goes back into the air so rapidly, that's bad news for humans."

"Is there any way to take the carbon out again?" I asked.

My father grinned. "There is," he said. "Lots of scientists are working on this problem, but can you guess one of the things that could help?"

Devon answered immediately. "More plankton."

"You got it."

My whole life I'd never understood what my father did all day—why he brought sample jars home and stored them in our refrigerator and why he cared so much about stuff we couldn't even see. How was it possible that something so important had been right in front of me this entire time and I'd never appreciated it?

"By studying plankton," Dad continued, "we can learn how to keep our oceans and our planet healthy for a long time to come." He paused. "So, on that note, let's get our nets into the water. Ana, what's our location and speed?"

She hollered back the answer and Devon wrote it on our clipboard.

"Jane?" Dad said, handing me the net. "Do you want to do the honors?"

Dad had rigged up a pulley system for raising and

lowering the net. It jutted out from the side of the boat. I fastened on the net and lowered it into the water, watching as it disappeared beneath the waves. Ana kept the boat moving at a steady speed and we timed how long the net was in the water. When Dad gave the signal, we hauled it back in again. The whole time I could hear the click of Devon's camera shutter.

"I've got a hose hooked up to the bilge," Dad said, "so we can get any plankton off the inside of the nets and into the jar. Devon, put that camera down and get your hands dirty."

Devon handed me the camera and clipboard. He hosed off the net until it looked clean and then we unhooked the jar and screwed on the cap.

"Store the sample in the cooler," Dad said. "We don't want to expose it to sunlight or heat. Then let's throw our net in again."

We worked steadily, taking sample after sample at different depths and locations, labeling each jar, and I found that my attention was so focused on what we were doing that I didn't even notice the whip of the wind, the cresting of the boat, or the gray clouds overhead. That is, I didn't notice until Elle lurched out of her seat and threw up off the port side.

"Enough already," Mom snapped. "You have plenty of

seawater. Your guests are miserable. Let's go home, for god's sake."

Looking around, I noticed that Erik had stopped talking and sat with his head between his knees. Dad glanced at me and Devon, but finally he nodded. "I guess that's enough for today. Jane, pull in the net and I'll tell Ana we're heading back."

I worked the pulley just like Dad had shown me. When the net was out of the water, dangling in the air, I leaned forward to haul it on board.

At that exact moment two things happened. One was that we got smacked by a large wave that lifted the boat up and then slapped us down again. The other was that *The Clam* lurched sharp to the starboard side. Under normal circumstances, a sharp turn like that wouldn't have hurt a thing.

But these weren't normal circumstances. In one second flat I'd gone head over heels, landing with a splash in the bitter cold of the Atlantic Ocean.

CHAPTER SIXTEEN

*Y*ou'd think what I'd remember most about falling overboard would be the shock of the freezing water or the briny taste of the saltwater that left me spluttering for air. But no. What I remember most was my mother's blood-curdling scream.

I'd always thought it was silly that Dad made me wear a life jacket even though I could swim, but as the waves towered over me, I understood why. Swimming in the cove was a lot different from trying to stay afloat at sea. My heart pounded in my chest and I fought back panic as I was lifted up and plunged down.

I'm okay. The life jacket is keeping me up.

I repeated the words like a mantra, watching as *The Clam* slowed down and turned back toward me. *Dad will save me,* I thought. *I know he will.*

Then someone dove overboard, but it wasn't Dad.

It was Erik.

Erik landed with a splash a little ways from me. I could see his bright orange life vest bobbing on the water and heard him gasping for air.

"Hang on, Jane!" he spluttered. "I'm coming!"

I kept treading water, my whole body thrumming with adrenaline. Dad threw a life ring in my direction, but I couldn't reach it.

"Swim, sprite!" Dad hollered.

I forced my shocked limbs into motion, swimming as hard as I could against the waves. Ana had slowed the engine to a crawl and she angled *The Clam* toward me. Close enough to reach me, but not too close in case we collided.

Finally, I grabbed the ring, holding on tight to the cold, hard plastic, and Dad pulled me over to the boat. I could hear his deep voice, calm and reassuring, calling out to Ana.

"Steady now. Steady."

Then his strong hands gripped my arms and hauled me up and over, onto the deck. I landed in a wet, shaking mess on the boat's floor. Mom ran over and hugged me so hard I thought my ribs might crack.

"Don't lose sight of Erik," Dad called to Ana.

Elle and Devon pointed in the distance.

"There he is!"

"Over there!"

Ana kept the boat moving forward until Erik was close by, and then Dad tossed the life ring once, twice . . . Erik rose and fell with every wave and my mother's face was dead white.

Finally, Erik grabbed hold of the ring and Dad hauled him up. Once he was on board, Erik lay on his back next to me and my mother fell over him, sobbing. Then, so quick that none of us saw it coming, she turned on my father and flew at him.

"They could have died!" she screamed, pummeling him with her fists. "You had to take everyone out on your *stupid* boat to do your *stupid* science, and . . . Jane could have died! You didn't even jump in after her."

"That wouldn't have helped the situation," Dad said. "Jane had on a life jacket, and what she needed was the life ring, not—"

Mom pounded on his chest. "No. *No, no, no!* For once, don't think with your head. Our *daughter* was out there." She jabbed her finger in the direction of the ocean with its dark, cresting waves.

"Calm down."

"I won't," she hollered. "You're always telling me to calm down."

"Mom," I said, "I wasn't in any—"

"Stay out of it, Jane," Mom snapped. She turned to Dad.

"I can't believe I ever left Jane with you! All you care about is this . . . this . . ." Mom sputtered, unable to come up with the right words. She made a sweeping gesture toward our water samples.

I wanted to holler back at her, but I was shivering so hard, I couldn't make my jaw work. Elle found an old wool blanket in the cab and wrapped it around my shoulders as Devon hovered nearby.

"Susan," Dad warned, "this isn't the time or place for this discussion. Jane and Erik are fine. Erik never should've jumped in—"

Mom cut him off. "They're *not* fine. What if they catch pneumonia?" She burst into tears. "This is all your fault, Emmett. Your. Fault."

"Actually," Elle said, "I'm the one who bumped into Ana while she was steering. The boat wouldn't have lurched like that if I'd worn sensible shoes."

"I don't want to hear it!" Mom hollered, and I could tell that knocked Elle off her guard. "We wouldn't be out here if it weren't for him."

"I'm the one who insisted he take us," Erik mumbled, his teeth chattering as much as mine.

"I don't care," Mom growled. "This is the second time I could've lost my child. There will *not* be a third."

"We'll talk about this later, Susan," Dad said. I could see the tension in his jaw as he leaned over me, rubbing my shoulders. "You okay, sprite?"

"I'm fine," I said, even though I was super cold.

Dad nodded. "We're going home."

When he'd gone into the cab, I stood up and handed Erik the blanket. "Here. You can have it. Thanks for jumping in after me."

Mom took off her sweatshirt and thrust it at me. "Put this on."

It wasn't worth arguing. I slipped the sweatshirt over my head and walked to the back of the boat. Devon slid up beside me.

"Are you really okay?" he asked.

I nodded. "Dad did the right thing, you know." I don't know why I felt the need to defend my father, but I did.

"I know," Devon said. "Your mom's pretty mad, though."

That was the truth. I could feel the emotion radiating off her in waves. She was crying again, huddled beside Erik, sharing the wool blanket. Her scream still echoed in my ears. Dad always said that Mom cared about me, but this was the first time I'd felt like it was true.

I stared at Dad, Ana, and Elle, the three of them clumped together in *The Clam*'s cab as if they were trying to stay as far away from Mom and Erik as possible. Ana was rubbing Dad's back and Elle still looked seasick.

"Does your father live in Wales?" The words slipped out before I could think them over. Devon startled, and at first I thought he wasn't going to answer, but at last he shook his head.

"No. He took a job in London." He paused. "I think he might have a girlfriend there."

"Do you ever wish you were with him instead of your mom?"

Devon shrugged. "I did at first. But now . . . mostly, I wish things hadn't changed in the first place. I miss Wales. Miss my friends. But I'm angry at *both* of my parents, not just Dad."

I had the strangest urge to hold his hand. I couldn't imagine leaving Whickett Harbor because my parents couldn't work out their problems. Maybe Maine wasn't the most glamorous place on earth, but it was *my* place.

Unfortunately, Devon was right: My mother was furious, and when Mom got mad, there was no telling what she'd do next.

CHAPTER SEVENTEEN

$\mathscr{R}$ight before the hurricane hit, the whole of Whickett Harbor had been silent and still. The sky was clear and blue, but there'd been an ominous feeling.

Sunday felt just like that—the quiet before the storm.

Dad took me and Devon into the lab to analyze the samples we'd taken. He showed us how to enter the data and chart it with the previous samples. Ana stayed at our house all day even though she didn't usually work on Sundays, and Kitty and Granny V came over for dinner so they could hear all about my "scrape with death." No matter how many times I tried to explain that I hadn't been in any actual danger, they refused to believe me.

"I was wearing a life jacket!" I said for the hundredth time, but Kitty just shook her head.

"What if you'd floated away? Or gotten attacked by a shark?"

I sighed. Honestly, it was hard to concentrate. Mom had called that morning to say that Erik had a cold—a result of his plunge into the Atlantic, she'd implied—and she needed to stay at their cabin to nurse him. She'd spoken to Dad, not me, and I'd only heard grunts from his side of the conversation. Twice he'd said, "We'll talk about this later, Susan."

What was *this*?

All day, I'd waited to see the little silver convertible pull into the driveway, thinking Mom would leave Erik for a few minutes so she could check on me, but she hadn't come.

That evening, when my father came in to say good night, I was already tucked into my soft, worn quilt with the fabric bunched beneath my chin. The small lamp beside my bed cast a dim glow. Ana had made the base out of a jar full of buttons, and I loved looking at all the shapes and colors through the glass.

Dad sat down on the edge of my bed and leaned over to turn off the light, but I stopped him.

"Dad? Mom is really angry. What do you think she'll do?"

There was a long pause. Too long. Then Dad shook his head. "You need to stop worrying about your mother. If she's angry, it's with me, not you. I know this has been a lot of upheaval in a short time, but your mom and Erik are only here for one more week, and then life will go back to normal."

Dad pushed the hair away from my forehead. "Your mother isn't one of the villains from your stories, you know, Jane. I realize she hasn't been the greatest mom, but she does have a heart. For all her faults, I believe she wants what's best for you. Give her a chance, sprite. A real one. She wants to be a better mom, and she's got one more week to make that happen."

Maybe Dad was right. By this time next week, Mom and Erik would be on a plane heading back to Hollywood. Would I miss them? Would they miss me?

Reluctantly, I nodded.

"Good girl." Dad kissed me on the forehead and shut off the light.

School was interminable on Monday. I sat at my desk staring at the clock, listening to Miss Bates prattle on. Her habit of interrupting herself seemed worse than usual, grating on my nerves. When the bell finally rang, Kitty and I gathered our things and headed home together, following the well-worn path.

"Matthew, Devon, and Caroline are coming over today,"

Kitty said. "Their mother is going to drop them off in an hour, after Caroline's music lesson. Did you know she's taking piano from Ms. Marianne?"

I shook my head, but my mind was only half focused on what Kitty had said.

"Do you want to come over too?"

Honestly, I wasn't sure I could tolerate Caroline's sneering today. Maybe I was catching Erik's cold, or maybe I was simply tired because I'd tossed and turned all night, but my whole body felt heavy.

"Sorry," I said. "I think I'm just going to curl up on the couch with Ana and put in a movie."

"Okay," Kitty said. "If you change your mind . . ."

We'd reached the place where the path split. We said goodbye and I watched as Kitty jogged up to her house before I set off across the field of blueberry bushes. When I got home, I stopped in my tracks.

Mom's convertible sat in the driveway.

I forced myself to move again. The kitchen door opened with a rusty squeak and I stepped inside, setting my backpack beside the island. Mom came around the corner and beamed when she saw me.

"Jane! You're finally home!"

"What are you doing here? Where's Ana?" I glanced around the kitchen, but Mom just laughed.

"You don't need a babysitter when your mother is here."

That was completely untrue. I needed Ana double.

"How's Erik?"

Mom frowned. "Still has a fever. But that's okay because it will give us some girl time."

"Girl time?"

Mom stepped aside and waved both arms toward the dining room. "Ta-da!" She paused, waiting for me to enter. "I thought we could get our nails done, so I looked for a spa, but of course . . . duh! . . . no spas anywhere near Whickett Harbor." Mom smacked her forehead with her palm as if she was trying to be funny, but it came out sounding disdainful. "But then I thought, why not make our own spa?"

Was she expecting me to jump up and down? Cheer? All I could do was stand there and stare. She'd cleaned our entire dining room so that it was spotless, and she'd laid out a dozen different bottles of nail polish and a huge makeup kit across the dining room table.

A whole mess of thoughts danced in my mind. Where were Dad's empty sample jars and his stacks of *Scientific American*? Where were my *Girl Power* magazines, writing journals, and the loose pages of notebook paper with my short stories and poems written on them?

I glanced around looking for our stuff and found it all

piled up in one corner behind the roll-top antique desk. I hated manicures, but I thought about what Dad had said the night before about my mother not being a villain from one of my stories. Maybe she was truly trying her best.

She'd strung up white lights around the dining room and had set two plastic mixing bowls of water on the floor. A fragrant, herbal smell saturated the air.

The room *did* look beautiful.

I took one hesitant step forward.

"Shall we get started?" Mom asked.

Mom had on jeans and one of those shirts that left her shoulders bare. Her dark hair—the same exact shade as mine—was pulled into a messy bun, and for one of the few times since she'd arrived in Whickett Harbor, she wasn't wearing heels. I'd rarely ever seen her look so casual. When I visited her in California, she always looked like a movie star. Even at bedtime, she wore matching silk pajama ensembles.

It was her scuffed-up cross trainers that convinced me to give her a chance. Maybe this was the Mom who Dad had fallen in love with. I'd always wanted to meet *her*.

"Okay," I said, taking off my old sneakers and socks. "Let's get started."

Mom grinned as she slipped off her shoes. She carefully rolled up both of her pant legs. "There's nothing like a spa treatment to relax you before—" Mom's words cut off and I wondered what she'd been about to say.

"Before what?"

"Dinner," she said, adding a little shrug at the end.

I sat down at the dining room table and eased my left foot into the plastic mixing bowl. The water was the same temperature as bath water and whatever she'd added made my foot feel tingly.

"This is nice."

Mom smiled. "Isn't it? I swear, if I don't have my weekly spa treatment, I'm a bear." She made a growly face and claw-hands. "Roar!"

Okay. That was just wrong. Sometimes adults were so embarrassing, it was hard to look at them.

"Did you do spa treatments with Granny when you were my age?"

"You think I did this with Granny?" Mom laughed. "Oh, honey. No. My mother and I didn't do anything together."

She left it at that. I'd met my grandmother several times, but Granny wasn't exactly what you'd call friendly. Granny didn't like children. Or babies. Or kittens. Or rainbows. She did have show horses, though, and she liked them just fine.

Mom and I settled in at the dining room table and the sounds of the B&B surrounded us as we soaked our feet.

The quiet ticking of the grandfather clock. The hum of the old refrigerator in the kitchen. A bumblebee buzzing against the window pane.

I scrambled for something to say, but all I came up with was more of the same. "So, how is Granny, anyway?"

I got a card at every holiday like clockwork, and she always wrote that she intended to visit—she'd see me soon and catch up with all her old friends in Whickett Harbor— but I'd always known those were empty words. I could count the number of times Granny had visited Whickett Harbor on one hand and have five fingers left over.

"She's fine," Mom said, looking surprised that I'd asked. "She's getting older now and can't get out like she used to. She can't understand why I don't move to Alabama to take care of her." Mom huffed. "I told her that perhaps her horses should have that responsibility."

My eyes must have showed my surprise, because Mom sighed.

"I know you've never understood why I left your father, Jane, but a big part of it was that I couldn't stand to compete with yet another species and lose. That's part of what I love about Erik. He adores *me*."

"How did you and Erik meet?" I asked.

"Mutual friends in the movie business. He took me to this

expensive restaurant on our first date—the kind you can't get into without pulling strings—and we talked for hours. And guess what." Mom leaned in as if she was telling me an important secret. "He hates horses. Had a riding accident as a child."

I laughed. "How long have you guys been dating?"

Mom gave an excited shimmy. "Eight months. Longest relationship I've had since your father."

It stung that Mom had never once mentioned Erik when we talked on the phone. Mostly she forgot to call, but when we did talk, our conversations were always the same. School, movie sets, her amazing job, how quickly she needed to hurry off . . . But I let it slide. Today, I was magnanimous Jane. Seeing the world from all points of view Jane.

"How long have you been engaged?"

"It'll be a month tomorrow!"

A tiny frown toyed at the edges of my magnanimous lips. Somehow, I'd gotten the impression that the engagement had *just* happened. My breathing was shaky, but Mom was oblivious.

"His proposal was so romantic," Mom gushed. "We were walking on the beach, and he reached down to the sand and pretended to pick something up. He had the ring in the palm of his hand the whole time, of course. Then he said, 'Look what I found. Guess you'll have to marry me.'"

"That *is* romantic." I could give him that much.

Mom reached over to examine the various bottles of nail polish. "What color do you want?" she asked. "Cotton Candy Pink? Raspberry Surprise?"

The truth was, I wouldn't be caught dead in either of those colors. I hated nail polish, but I gritted my teeth remembering how magnanimous I was being.

I picked Silver Sparkle, which was almost clear but was designed to make it look like you had glitter on your fingernails. How bad could that be?

Mom chose Passionate Peach.

As we applied our colors, I thought about how I could describe the toxic smell coming from the nail polish bottles, or the cool, almost heavy sensation of the polish.

I wondered if Mom ever thought about how to describe things. After all, she was a screenwriter. We ought to have writing in common, so how come we never talked about that? I opened my mouth to ask, but Mom took her foot out of the mixing bowl. Soapy water dripped onto our braided rug making a foot-sized stain as Mom twirled her nail polish bottle between her fingers.

"You see, Jane," she said. "I really like Erik."

Well, I'd hope so, considering they're engaged.

"That's great," I said, oblivious to what was coming.

"He's an incredible man. Successful. Generous. Kind. And what Erik wants"—she paused—"is a family. He's always wanted kids."

Every muscle in my body went taut.

"I know I'm still young," Mom said, "but honestly, I don't want a baby. You know better than anyone, Jane . . . I'm not exactly Mother of the Year." She sighed. "But I'd like to change that. I'd like us to be a family—you, me, and Erik—and if that's going to happen, then you'd need to be with us in California more often."

My stomach twisted.

"You'd like that, wouldn't you?" Mom prodded. "You've got to be getting tired of Whickett Harbor by now. As a girl gets older, she needs to stretch her wings. Explore new places. Be around different people. And as a young writer, the chance to be on a movie set . . ." Mom made one of those gestures that indicated the rest of the sentence was a foregone conclusion.

"What are you saying?" I asked, my pulse racing.

Mom hesitated. She finger-combed her dark hair and pursed her lips. "I was thinking maybe you'd want to come live with us for a while. Wouldn't it be great to have a change?"

I dropped the fingernail brush, my heart slamming

against my rib cage. It made a glittery smear across the dining room table. "Live with you? In California?"

"Yes." Mom nodded. "Erik and I made a decision after your accident. We're going to file for custody. We love you, Jane. You may not know it yet, but we'd be doing you a favor, getting you out of this backwater town."

I pushed away from the table so hard that my entire basin of herbal water spilled over the floor.

"No." I ground the word between my teeth.

"Jane?"

"No!" I repeated. "You think you and Erik *love* me? He's barely met me and you don't even know me well enough to know that I hate nail polish and I hate pink and I hate *you*."

My feet had carried me out of the dining room before I even registered where I was going. I scooped up my old rubber waders near the front door because those were the only shoes I could slip on without stopping, and then I headed for the blueberry field. Mom hollered after me, but I didn't turn around.

Not even once.

CHAPTER EIGHTEEN

$\mathcal{T}$o get to Kitty's house required a long walk through a boggy field of scrub brush—almost a mile—and walking sockless in waders made it seem even longer. My feet hurt and my eyes were filled with angry tears, so I could hardly see where I was going, but that didn't matter. I knew the way. By the time I arrived in Kitty's backyard, emerging out of the brush like some sort of swamp monster, I was covered in mud and my eyes were sore and bloodshot.

Granny V was out back, hanging laundry on a clothesline so it could air dry, but she took one look at me and dropped her laundry basket.

"Jane! Good gracious! Is everything okay?"

"No." I hiccupped. "Is Kitty home?"

"Of course. Come inside."

Granny V hugged me, then ushered me in and called for Kitty, who came down a few minutes later, accompanied by three unwelcome faces: Matthew, Devon, and Caroline. I'd forgotten they'd be there.

Caroline's eyes widened as she took in my appearance.

"Oh my god. Look at her," she whispered to Devon, just loud enough for me to hear. "Are those galoshes? And she's got mud up to her knees."

"Jane!" Kitty squealed. "What happened to you?"

Devon took a step forward, studying my red, puffy eyes. "Are you okay?" His expression was softer than I'd ever seen it before, and he bit his lower lip as he waited for my response.

"Fine," I managed. "I'll be fine." I turned to Kitty. "Could I talk to you alone?"

She nodded. "Outside. At the swing."

We headed out to her yard and each took one side of the tire swing. Kitty waited for me to talk.

"Mom is filing for custody." The minute the words were out of my mouth, I burst into tears. Kitty made a horrified squeal.

"No! She can't! She's barely seen you all these years, and now she thinks she can—"

"Take me away. That's exactly what she thinks." I wiped my nose on my sleeve. "She doesn't even want me. Erik is the one who wants a kid. Mom is just trying to make him happy."

Kitty shook her head. "That's awful, Jane. We have to stop this."

"I know, but I don't see how. There's two of them and only one of Dad. Mom's going to tell everyone how I got lost during the hurricane and fell off the boat. She used to be an actress, so she'll lay it on thick with the judge and make it sound like Dad doesn't take care of me."

I burst into a new flood of tears.

"No. We can't let this happen," Kitty said. "We need to set your father up with Elle right away. Then at least they'll be even. Plus, maybe Elle would pitch in for an expensive lawyer."

I rested my face against the scratchy rope and felt the tiny fibers scraping my cheek. "I don't know, Kitty. I don't think judges care who someone is dating."

"Well, your mom and Erik aren't married either. Have they even set a date for the wedding?"

"Not as far as I've heard, although I'd probably be the last one to know. But Dad will never ask anyone out. That kind of thing just doesn't occur to him."

Now Kitty burst into tears.

"Maybe you could change Erik's mind about having a kid," she sobbed. "If you're a total brat, he'll decide he doesn't want you to live with them."

I thought that over, but Erik seemed like the kind of guy

who wouldn't let anything stand in the way of what he wanted. He'd jumped off the boat to save me without any hesitation, and even though he hadn't actually needed to do it, that still seemed pretty committed to me.

"You could at least talk to your father about dating someone," Kitty said when I didn't respond. "If you lay out the facts for him, maybe he'll be willing to change. I know he doesn't want to lose you, Jane."

"I'll talk to him," I said, "but he'll just say we don't need to resort to desperate measures. Dad never thinks it's time for desperate measures."

"You can't give up hope," Kitty pleaded. "Not until we've tried everything." She flung her arms around me and we hugged until Granny V called us inside.

"I phoned your house, Jane," Granny V said. "I spoke to your mother. She's all in a flutter." She sighed. "I spoke to your father as well. He's on his way home, and he said that Ana will pick you up shortly."

I nodded. A hug from Ana was exactly what I needed right now.

We went in and sat at the dining room table. Matthew and Caroline were huddled over Kitty's laptop, but Devon hadn't joined them. He stood nearby, staring at me and Kitty. Glowering, really. I couldn't say why, but something in my gut told me he'd been eavesdropping.

I held back the flood of tears that wanted to burst out again. I wouldn't cry while Devon was watching. Instead, I lifted my chin and waited for Ana to arrive. Outside, the sunset had colored the horizon in deep shades of red, and the autumn leaves stood out in sharp relief. When I heard the rattle of Ana's truck in the driveway, I stood up and hugged Kitty goodbye.

I hugged Granny V too, and she told me what she always said whenever I was upset: "Remember Jane, you must let your courage rise with every attempt to intimidate it." That was her favorite Jane Austen quote.

"Thanks," I murmured. I walked outside and was just about to step into Ana's truck, when Devon ran out of Kitty's house.

"Wait!" he hollered, waving an envelope in the air. "I almost forgot to give this to you. It's for your father. From my mom."

I stared at the envelope, wondering what could be inside. "What is it?"

Devon shrugged. "How should I know?"

I didn't have it in me to argue. Not tonight. I took the envelope and got in Ana's truck, shutting the door behind me and watching in the rearview mirror as she pulled away from Kitty's house and Devon's figure faded from view.

CHAPTER NINETEEN

*A*na let me sit in silence the whole ride home, but I could tell by the look on her face that she knew what had happened, and for the first time that I could remember, she looked scared. Her knuckles were white on the steering wheel and her jaw was tight.

When we pulled up to the B&B, we could hear Mom and Dad fighting—loud and furious. If there was one good thing about having divorced parents, it was that I usually didn't have to hear them argue.

"Don't go inside, Jane," Ana said. "Not yet."

We sat in my driveway with the windows up, but that didn't prevent us from hearing bits and pieces every time their voices rose.

"*. . . can't keep me away from my daughter . . .*"

"*. . . never think about anyone other than yourself . . .*"

"*I'll spend every penny I have on lawyers if that's what it takes . . .*"

Ana reached over and stroked my hair. "Jane?"

"Yeah?" I sniffed.

"Want to go somewhere else?"

I nodded and Ana started the engine again. She pulled out and drove toward the pier without my even having to ask. We parked at the Clam Shack and walked along the dock until we reached the very end, and then we sat with our legs dangling over the water.

The moon was full and it cast a yellow glow on the ocean's surface. It was too early to see many stars, but that didn't matter. All I wanted was to watch the waves rolling in, one after the other, as far as the eye could see.

When Ana and I pulled back into the driveway an hour later with fried clams and French fries from the Clam Shack, the house was quiet and still. The kitchen lights were on, but my mother's rental car was gone and I breathed a sigh of relief.

Before we could even get inside, my father stepped out to meet us. Even in the darkness, I could tell he didn't look like himself. There was a fierceness about him that I'd never seen before. I tried to put my finger on what made me think of that word. Was it the length of his strides or the way his gaze never wavered?

When he reached me, he hugged me so hard, he lifted me

straight off my feet. Ana started to turn away to give us some privacy, but Dad pulled her in too, and the three of us stood in the driveway like that for a long time.

Finally, Dad let us both go.

"I brought dinner," Ana said. "I figured you wouldn't have thought about food."

Dad nodded and we headed in. We cleared the surface of the kitchen island and set out paper plates, tartar sauce, and ketchup while Ana pulled up our tall stools. It was as if the new cleaned-up version of our dining room was cursed, so without anyone saying it, we all knew that no one wanted to eat in there.

"Did you go to the pier?" Dad asked.

Ana nodded. "Figured you and Susan could use some time to sort things out."

Dad took a deep breath. "Jane," he said at last, "your mother shouldn't have done what she did. She knows you're upset and she said she'll give you some time, but sooner or later you'll have to talk things over with her. She's your mom, after all. You can't shut her out forever."

"Is she still going to file for custody?"

Dad gave a clipped nod.

"Then I *can* shut her out and I will," I said, feeling every muscle in my body go rigid. Dad and Ana exchanged looks, but finally he relented.

"Guess we'll revisit this when it's not so fresh," he said.

"You mean after Mom and Erik have filed the papers? Do you even have a lawyer, Dad?" I was betting Mom and Erik could afford a good one—top of the line—while Dad would probably end up using Mr. Bedard, who considered lawyering his second career after managing his Superette.

Dad shook his head. "Let me worry about that stuff."

"I'll pitch in," Ana said, real quiet, but I was pretty sure that Ana didn't have any money to spare.

"Both of you stop worrying," Dad said. "If Susan follows through, we'll fight this and we'll win." His deep, baritone voice sounded steady and sure, but his hand shook as it was reaching for a clam, so he thrust it into his pocket instead. Ana took a handful of clams and put them on his plate, and then she did the same for herself and for me so it would look like she was dishing them out for all of us.

If there was one thing I missed most about being a little kid, it was believing that my father was invincible. Now I could see the way the lines on his forehead had turned into deep grooves and the tension lingered in his eyes.

"It'll be fine," Dad said. "This is just another one of your mother's phases. She'll be over it by next week. Not that she doesn't love you, Jane. She truly does want to see you more often, but maybe you'll go out to California for an extra week or two in the summer next year."

Ana flipped her hair like a starlet. "California . . . home of beach volleyball, celebrity tours, and wax museums. Everything you love, Jane. How can you resist?"

Despite myself, I laughed. "Well, if I get to ride in a Hummer limousine, I might consider it."

"You mean my truck isn't good enough for you?" Dad said.

"It does smell like dead fish," Ana pointed out.

"Women." Dad shook his head. "So picky."

"Men," Ana countered. "So oblivious."

The very last thing I would've expected at the end of that night was to be sitting around my kitchen eating fried clams and laughing. When Ana finally left, it was after nine o'clock and we both watched her go. My eyes were sore and tired, the swollen lids still heavy from crying.

Dad threw out the last of the garbage and nodded toward the stairs. "All right, Ms. Jane. Up to bed. And don't keep yourself awake worrying, you hear? Everything will work out."

I stood on my tiptoes to kiss Dad's cheek, and that's when I felt the envelope shift in the back pocket of my jeans. I'd shoved it there after Devon gave it to me, but I took it out and handed it to Dad.

"What's this?"

"I don't know. Devon asked me to give it to you."

"How odd." Dad tore open the seal and slipped out a piece of fancy stationery. He took out his reading glasses, perched them on the bridge of his nose, and read aloud. "Dear Emmett . . . It was so nice of you to take us out on your boat. I'm sorry we all got sick. I'd love to see you again, and I'm hoping you might be my date to the Butterfly Ball. Your most ardent admirer, Elle."

Dad blinked several times in a row. "She's asking for . . . a date?" He tilted his head to one side and stared at the letter as if it were written in ancient hieroglyphics.

"She is," I said, my heart beating faster. "Are you going to say yes?"

Dad paused. "I don't know. I . . . It's been years since I went on a date. I didn't think anyone would be interested in me."

"Why would you say that?"

Dad shrugged. "After Susan left . . . all those things she said . . ." He paused and fixed me with a wry stare. "I know you'll find this shocking, but she claimed I could bore any woman to tears with my constant scientific babble."

I flushed. Then I took a deep breath. "Dad, you're a smart, attractive, interesting guy. I don't think Elle will be bored. In fact, I've been told on good authority that you're hot for an old guy."

"Me?! Who said that?"

"Kitty."

"Huh." Dad scratched his chin. "Then it must be true. She is the authority on all things good-looking."

I laughed. "Say yes, Dad? Please?"

Dad ran his fingers over the smooth wood of the kitchen counter. "I guess it couldn't hurt."

"Thank you!" I wrapped him in a hug.

"Now, don't go getting your hopes up. It's one date."

"I know, I know," I said, but for the first time since my mother's announcement, I felt hopeful. If I had the famous and powerful J. E. Fairfax on my side, even my mother's movie producer fiancé couldn't top that. I snatched the letter off the counter and kissed it.

Dad rolled his eyes. "I mean it, sprite. Don't go making up stories in your head about me and Elle getting married and living happily ever after. I know how that brain of yours works. Here's what's going to happen: We're going to stand around and watch you kids dance, and I'm going to try my hardest not to say the word *plankton*. That's hardly the stuff that romance is made of."

"Uh-huh." I kissed my father on the tip of his nose and sashayed out of the kitchen and up the stairs. It wasn't until I was already in my bedroom that I realized I still had the notecard in my hand. I read it again and admired the raised pink swirls on the front of the card and then I turned it over.

And that's when I saw it.

On the back of the notecard, there was a tiny little cat face with a brand name underneath. Hello Kitty.

CHAPTER TWENTY

The next day at school, I flung my arms around Kitty the moment I saw her. She'd just arrived and was hanging up her pink backpack in the locker area.

"You're in a surprisingly good mood," she said. "What was that for?"

"Because you're the best friend a girl could ever have."

Kitty preened at the compliment. "Yes, that's true." She paused. "But what exact best-friendish thing did I do most recently?"

I laughed. "The note," I prodded. "To my father."

"Note?" Kitty asked. "I didn't write your father a note."

"Oh, right." I winked. "Elle wrote the note asking my father out."

Kitty's jaw dropped. "J. E. Fairfax asked your father out? On a date?"

I was losing patience with this game. "Of course. As you well know, since you wrote the note."

"But I didn't," Kitty said, shaking her head. "I wish I had, but that never occurred to me."

"Well, if you didn't write it, then who did? It was written on one of your notecards. There was a Hello Kitty logo on the back."

"Maybe it really was from J. E. Fairfax. I'm not the only one who loves Hello Kitty, you know."

Somehow, I doubted that a best-selling author would use Hello Kitty notecards for her correspondence, but if she didn't write it and Kitty didn't write it . . . My eyes strayed across the room to where Matthew and Devon were quizzing each other on spelling words.

"Did Matthew write it?"

Kitty shook her head. "He and Caroline were with me the entire time." She gasped. "It must have been—"

"Devon?!" We both said his name at the same time and he looked up from across the room. Kitty waved, but I just stood there.

Was it possible? But why? If anyone had reason *not* to want our parents to get together, it was Devon. He hated it here in Whickett Harbor, and until very recently, I'd been convinced he hated me.

Miss Bates's voice rang out over the bustling hum of the classroom. "Okay, children . . . take your seats, please. We'll begin with the spelling test. Everyone take out a piece of paper and a pencil."

As Kitty and I made our way to our seats, my mind whirled. I couldn't help staring at Devon, but he was purposefully avoiding eye contact. My desk was three seats ahead of his and one row over, but when I sat down, I swore I could feel his eyes on me.

The only question was why.

It wasn't until lunch that I finally got to talk to Devon. It wasn't a lab day, so we'd followed the spelling test with a history lesson, and then the seventh graders had language arts. We sat in a circle reading aloud from our Greek mythology book, but I was distracted the entire time.

At lunch, Devon filed into the cafeteria with a clump of boys, and I wove my way through the lunch line until I was behind him. As soon as we'd both exited the line, I called out.

"Hey! Wait up!"

He stopped by the garbage bins and turned, holding his plastic tray more tightly. "Yes?"

There was no point beating around the bush. "Did you write the note to my father?"

Devon shrugged. "Matthew's right. Our mom needs to get out more. She's depressed, and when Mom is depressed, she does stuff like move us to another country so we can get a fresh start."

A wave of surprise and gratitude washed over me, but even though Devon was acting as if he hardly cared, I sensed the raw texture of his words.

"So," I said, matching his casual tone, "how will your mom react when my dad shows up to chaperone thinking it's a date?"

"I wrote a similar note to my mother. In fact, I gave it to her last night."

"Did you write the note from my father on the same pink Hello Kitty notecards?"

The corner of Devon's mouth twitched. "It was all I had available on short notice."

We both laughed, and then we caught ourselves. Since when did I stand around laughing with Devon Fairfax?

"Well, I guess I should go." He nodded toward the group of boys he usually sat with at lunch, but as he walked away, I called after him again.

"Wait. Did you develop the pictures from the boat trip yet?"

He turned and grinned. "Yes. They came out great. I got some good ones at the lab too."

I paused. "Well then, maybe we should start brainstorming for our article."

Devon lifted one brow. "Yeah?"

"That is . . . if you don't mind sitting with me instead of the boys."

Devon shrugged. "You'd sit with me instead of the girls?"

"It wouldn't be the worst thing in the world."

"Okay then." Devon set his tray down at one of the empty tables and I took the seat across from him. We both reached for our chocolate milks at the exact same time, and our hands touched, so we pulled away quick. I felt a hot blush spread across my cheeks and the bridge of my nose.

"Want to talk about something else before we discuss the article?" I asked.

"Like what?"

"If you've never been on a boat before and you didn't live near the coast in Wales, then how did you get interested in ocean science?"

"That's a long story."

I shrugged. "We've got time."

So that's how Devon and I ended up spending our lunch period together, talking and laughing the entire time. Turns out, he could be funny when you gave him a chance. I never would've guessed there was a sense of humor lurking under his sweater vests and ties.

We never did end up discussing our article.

And the odd thing was, I didn't even mind.

CHAPTER TWENTY-ONE

How to Make Plankton Interesting:

Add fur.

Make it bigger.

Give it ears and whiskers.

Cover it in rainbow sprinkles.

Give up. It's impossible.

That afternoon, I sat in my writing nook trying to create an article that wasn't flat-out boring. No luck. The crumpled-up pages of my botched attempts made a heap on the kitchen floor. Nothing was right, and I could already see the mock rejection letter in my head.

Dear Contributor,

Thank you for your wasted time and effort, but everything you wrote was dull and stupid. Your article sounded like a science text-book that no one would ever want to read.

Sincerely,

The Editorial Team

How could I make any of this feel important?

When I'd reached the point where my imaginary rejection letter made it impossible to write another word, I knew there was nothing else to do but sacrifice my pride and beg for help. Elle Fairfax didn't write science articles, but she was the only real writer I knew, so maybe, just maybe, if I tried one final time she'd give me some piece of advice that would make everything come clear. After all, I was working with her son on this project, so that had to count for something.

I gathered my courage, picked up the phone, and dialed the number that Devon had written on the clipboard along with our notes. The phone rang once, twice . . . I almost chickened out and hung up, but then I heard Elle's melodic voice.

"Hello?"

"Uh, hi . . ." My pulse raced. What should I say? What if she didn't want to help me? "This is Jane Brannen."

"Jane! How lovely to hear from you. Are you calling for Devon?"

"No. Actually, I . . ." Now that I finally had my chance, I could barely get the words out. "I was calling to talk to you—that is, if you're not busy and you don't mind." I sounded like Miss Bates. "I wanted to ask for some advice. About my science project. The one I'm doing with Devon."

I forced myself to keep talking. "You see, Devon took the pictures and I'm writing the article, only . . . I can't seem to get it right, and I thought . . . maybe . . ."

Elle made a knowing sort of noise. "You were hoping I might offer some insight?"

"Yes," I breathed. "Could you?" I paused. "I mean, I know you can't give out your very best secrets to just anyone, but . . ."

Elle chuckled. "My very best secrets, eh?" She paused. "Well, I couldn't give those out over the phone, but I'd be happy to speak with you in person. Why don't you come by with Devon after school tomorrow? I know he wants to show you his photos, and you could bring your rough draft of the article so we can talk shop."

My whole body flooded with excitement. "Really?"

"Really," Elle confirmed. "I'd love to have you visit. Plan to stay for dinner, Jane."

This was almost too much. I nodded like a bobble-head doll. "Thank you. Thank you so much."

When I hung up the phone I couldn't stop grinning. Even when my mother called right after I'd hung up, it didn't ruin my happiness.

"Jane," she said, sounding stern, "we need to talk. I've given you time, but—"

"No, Mom." I cut her off. "You've given me two days, but that isn't enough. I'll talk to you when I'm ready."

I could almost hear the whine forming in my mother's throat.

"Why do you even *need* time?" she wailed. "When I was your age I would've kissed the feet of someone who promised to take me away from here. I love you, Jane. You know I do. You're my daughter. And Erik is a good man. California is an amazing place to live. If you let us, we can give you the world."

The familiar flood of fear and anger threatened to pull me under, but I forced it back. "I know that's what you think," I said, "but I'm not ready to talk about this yet."

"When will you be ready?" Mom asked, sounding like a stubborn kid. "Erik and I are only here until Sunday," she reminded me, "and then we fly home."

I was well aware of when they flew home.

"Friday night," I said. "Give me until the Butterfly Ball. Matthew said Erik is helping with the cameras, so you'll be there too, right? We can talk about everything then."

"Jane," Mom said, "will you at least let me see you before then if I promise not to talk about custody?"

"No." My voice didn't waver even the tiniest bit. "I'm having dinner with the Fairfaxes tomorrow night and then on Thursday I need to write the article for my science project. I have a deadline. So, I'll see you Friday night. Take it or leave it."

There was stunned silence from my mother's end of the phone. Finally, she said, "I guess I'll take it, then."

"Good." I hung up.

Dad was working late, so Ana was home with me. She'd been pretending to dust our dining room ever since I'd called Elle, even though we both knew that vacuuming and dishes were as far as Ana's cleaning went.

Now she came around the corner and hugged me tight.

"Jane," she said, "I definitely should have gotten you that other necklace. You *are* an obstinate, headstrong girl, and I mean that as the best compliment ever."

CHAPTER TWENTY-TWO

$\mathcal{W}$ednesday after school I rode home with Caroline, Matthew, and Devon. According to Devon, the very first thing Caroline did when they got their dual citizenship was to get her driver's license. Her car was similar to my mother's rental car—small and sporty. Matthew sat in the front, and I sat in the back with Devon.

Driving with Caroline was a bit like riding a roller coaster. Twice, my butt flew off the seat when we hit a bump. When we finally pulled up in front of the Penmore Estate, I tumbled out as soon as possible.

"That was a pretty smooth ride," Devon said. "I think she was being extra careful because you're in the car."

"Definitely," Matthew agreed. "We didn't endanger a single pedestrian."

Caroline gave us an evil glare. "Shut it, pipsqueaks. I would think those who can't drive should simply be grateful to those of us who can."

I supposed she had a point.

"So what's it like to live here?" I asked as we walked up the front path. "Was your old house this big?"

Devon snorted. "Our old house was practically a cottage compared to this monstrosity."

"This one does echo a lot," Matthew said. "It's kind of like living in a museum."

"I don't know what you two are talking about," Caroline said, swinging open the front door. "I love this place. I wouldn't want to live someplace shabby."

Was it my imagination, or did she look pointedly at me?

I didn't have time to worry about Caroline's insult because Elle arrived, looking stylish in a cream-colored pantsuit, sweeping down the spiral stairs like a queen. She fussed over her kids, asking about their day at school and reminding them to get a healthy snack, and then she turned to me.

"Jane," she said, "you and I have important business to discuss. Secrets to divulge." She winked. "Did you bring your rough draft?"

I nodded.

"Well then, let's not waste any time." She gestured for me to follow her up the stairs. "I already have tea laid out in my office."

Even though I'd seen Elle's office during the tour, I hadn't gotten a good look. Now I sat in one of the big leather chairs and studied everything around me. *This,* I thought, *is exactly what an author's office ought to look like.* It was spacious and regal, with a huge mahogany desk in the center of the room, and most importantly, the walls were lined from floor to ceiling with books. There was even a wooden ladder set at an angle so you could reach the top shelves.

I sighed contentedly.

"So," Elle said, "shall I read what you have so far?"

"I guess." I handed her the crumpled pages of my most recent draft. "It's not very good. I did hours of research, but it's hard to make all the facts sound interesting."

Elle nodded. "Here, have some tea and biscuits while you wait." She took a seat behind the huge desk and began to read. I picked up a biscuit—which was actually a cookie— and poured myself a cup of tea even though I never drank tea. But when someone with an accent suggests you should have tea and a biscuit, it's hard to refuse.

There's nothing worse than watching someone read what you've written. I felt as if my guts were being stretched like dough that had been rolled too flat. My mind said that of course she would find things wrong with my article, but my heart was secretly hoping she'd love every word.

I nibbled at the biscuit—it was a dry, dull sort of cookie

that tasted like paste in my mouth. Then I sipped at my tea, but it was bitter, so I added two more cubes of sugar, trying not to clank the spoon too loudly as I stirred.

After what felt like an eternity, Elle set down my pages.

"You have talent, Jane," she said. "This is good writing."

I waited for her to add "for your age," but she didn't. My heart leaped.

"But I can see what the problem is," she continued. "There's something missing."

My heart sank. "What is it?"

"The secret to great writing, of course," Elle said. "Isn't that what you came here to find out?" She raised one eyebrow knowingly.

Ah-ha! So there *was* a secret. My heart pounded and I chewed on my lower lip trying to contain my excitement.

"What is it?" I whispered.

"The secret," said Elle, "is both so simple that you won't need to lift a finger to accomplish it, and so difficult that you will never be able to force the outcome."

What kind of riddle was that?

"You must fall in love."

"Fall in love?" I echoed. I'd been disappointed by Elle's advice before, but this had to be the worst one yet.

She nodded. "Yes. It's one of the great mysteries of

writing, and no one can quite say how it happens, but somehow your audience will know if you're in love with what you write. They will sense whether you've poured your heart into your words or merely used your brain. If you've only used your brain, chances are they'll put down your work without much thought, but if you've used your heart, their hearts will beat in sync with what you've written."

My tea and biscuits sat abandoned. Elle wasn't just terrible at giving advice; it was possible that she was flat-out crazy. "But . . . how do I . . . do that?" I asked, trying to be polite. "I've never been in love."

Elle chuckled. "Well, what's the opposite of love?"

"Hate?"

"Ah. A common mistake. But no." Elle's expression was serious, as if we weren't having the weirdest conversation ever. "Two people can hate each other passionately, yet that can be the prelude to very intense love. In fact, that's the basis for half of my romance novels!" She laughed. "Try again."

I shook my head. I couldn't come up with anything else.

"Fear," Elle said at last. "Fear is the opposite of love because when we're afraid, that's when we don't tell the truth. We try to be something we're not. And Jane," she said, very seriously, "writers must never lie."

"But don't we lie every time we tell a story?"

Elle looked surprised. "Of course not," she said. "The surface might be made up, but the center must always be the truth as we see and feel it. That's storytelling, not lying. An important distinction."

"I'm sorry," I said. "I'm still not sure I'm getting this."

Elle paused. "In these pages, Jane, I'd say that you're trying to sound like someone else. One of those dry, stuffy experts who writes textbooks."

I nodded. "I want people to think I'm an expert."

"Are you an expert?"

I shook my head.

"Then you must not lie, Jane."

"But if I'm not an expert, why should anyone read what I'm writing?"

"They'll read it because your heart is in it." She fixed me with a hard stare. "Do you love plankton?"

I scrunched up my nose. "Kind of? I mean, it's interesting and it does good things for us. But . . ."

"But . . ." Elle prompted.

"Mostly I love my dad," I admitted. "Plankton makes me think of him."

"Good," Elle said. "Why does it make you think of your father?"

"Well, because of his job and because it's something most people take for granted, but they shouldn't, because without it, we wouldn't have clean air to breathe. It would be easy to take my dad for granted, but without him . . ."

I thought about my mom and Erik, and how they'd never be able to see my father the way I saw him. To them, he'd always be plain and dull, but to me he was everything.

Without him, I couldn't breathe.

I gasped. "Maybe I *do* get it."

Elle smiled. "I knew you would." She sat back. "Now, tell me what is really at the heart of your article, Jane. Not what someone else would say, but what *you* believe. Don't overthink it; just tell it to me plain."

"The article is about plankton," I said, "but it's also about all of the small things in life that aren't glamorous?"

Elle waved me on, encouraging me to continue.

"I guess it's about the things no one celebrates. Learning to see what's always been there, even if we've never appreciated it before."

"Exactly!" Elle smiled. "And whose life will you focus on as you tell this story?"

I almost said "everyone's?" but then I remembered the very first piece of advice Elle Fairfax had ever given me. *Write what you know.*

"My own?"

"Brilliant girl."

A nervous feeling made my stomach churn. I'd never intended to write about myself.

"No one ever said that good writing was easy," Elle chided, studying my expression. "Falling in love again and again? Spilling your heart all over the page?" She sighed. "But if you're really meant to be a writer, you'll tell the truth as you know it. Every time." She handed my papers back to me. "So, there you are. I've passed along my very best secret. Now it's your turn. Tell your story, Jane. *Your* story. If you do, I promise, that will be an article I'll want to read."

CHAPTER TWENTY-THREE

It was amazing how much easier the article was to write after that. I spent the rest of the evening with Devon, looking at his photographs from our boat trip, and the whole time my mind raced with ideas.

There was a photo of *The Clam* moored to the dock. It was just a secondhand lobster boat, but for ten years it had been used for scientific expeditions that might help the entire human species. I found a picture of Dad's callused hands holding the plankton net with confidence. Another one showed Ana standing behind the wheel of the boat, her hair falling out of a messy bun. A smudge of dirt streaked the side of her face as she beamed at the camera.

I leafed through every one of Devon's photos and found pictures he'd taken ever since he'd first moved here. There was a picture of the Whickett Harbor sign, which had fallen half off during the hurricane so you had to read it sideways. And there were Hollis and Louise Adams standing outside the *Clam Shack* holding their brand-new baby boy. There was Miss Bates sitting at her desk in front of the classroom staring dreamily into space. There was Pop sound asleep behind the counter at the café. And there were me and Devon standing beside the scientists who worked with my father, all of us crowded around the spectroscopes at the lab.

Every picture was special, and I knew just what I wanted to say about them.

That night I stayed up writing until one in the morning. I sat in my writing nook until my flashlight burned out, long after Dad had told me to go to bed. This time, the words flowed easily, and even though I ended up doing just as many drafts as I'd done the day before, they felt different. I knew that the heart of the article was there—beating strong and true.

I also knew I wouldn't give up until I'd gotten it right, because Elle was correct.

Somewhere along the way, I'd finally fallen in love with plankton.

Love was exhausting.

My eyes were heavy the next morning, but the final draft of the article was tucked in my backpack when I headed to school.

I'd asked Dad to drive me so I could get there early. I'd bought a tri-fold poster board, and Devon and I had agreed that we'd meet in the morning before school. We'd mount the article in the center board and glue the best photos around it. Along the top, we'd draw out instructions for how to do plankton sampling, and along the bottom we'd show the graph from Dad's study, adding our own research.

Dad dropped me off, kissing the top of my head. "Good luck, sprite. Hope Miss Bates appreciates all of your hard work."

"Thanks," I said, but I was surprised to find that I didn't care whether Miss Bates gave me a good grade. Even if she gave us an F I'd still do the project again.

I hurried out of the truck. The day was cool and the sky was a soft shade of blue. I stood for a moment, looking up at the clouds. A few minutes later, Devon appeared at my elbow.

"Hi," he said. "Did you get the article done?"

I nodded, fishing the papers out of my backpack. "Want to read it?"

"Of course." He took the pages, went over to the front steps of the school, sat down, and started to read. "Falling in Love with Plankton: How One Girl on the Coast of Maine Learned to Care About the Ocean."

I watched Devon's face as he read, feeling just as nervous as I had when his mother read my first attempt. I had to stifle the urge to interrupt him. Was that a smile? A grimace? Was he bored? Interested? Did he wish it had been his job to write the article? I could barely stand still.

When he finally finished, Devon set the pages on his lap. He was quiet for a long time while I shifted my weight from one foot to the other.

"Well?" I said at last.

"It's all about you."

A rush of mortification made my face heat up. *He hated it.* He was going to say that I needed to start over. Why had I ever thought I should make the article about me? "I'm sorry. I can try again if—"

"No," Devon said, the word crisp like the morning air. "You misunderstood. The article is beautiful. I was just surprised because I thought it would be facts and stuff like that, but instead it's personal. Everything people need to know is still there, only now they can see why this stuff matters. Because it matters to *you*."

I caught my breath. "Are you sure? I can change the title. It could say 'How Two Kids Learned to Care About the Ocean,' except you already understood why that's important." I paused. "I was also thinking maybe we could submit the article to *Girl Power* magazine. If they published it, then even more people would learn about why we need to take care of the ocean, and maybe they'd do things differently."

Devon stared at me with a funny expression.

I winced. "I'd give you credit too, of course. Maybe there's a boy power magazine we could send it to? It was just an idea. We don't have to—"

He cut me off. "I love it. You already give me plenty of credit in the article, and I think reaching more people is a brilliant idea."

"Are you sure? Because—"

"Jane," Devon blurted out, "will you go to the Butterfly Ball with me?"

My eyes widened in surprise. Where had *that* come from? "You mean . . . as your date?"

Devon nodded. "I know you hated me when we first met," he said, "but since then . . . if you still don't like me, just say so and I'll never bring this up again, but if your feelings have changed . . ."

"But I thought you hated *me*."

Devon blushed. "No. Actually, I think you're the most interesting girl I've ever met."

The words took my breath away. Stuck-up Devon Fairfax liked me? Except, maybe I hadn't actually thought of him as stuck-up for a long time now. Not since he'd written that fake note to my father. Maybe even before that.

"Yes," I said at last. "I'd love to go to the ball with you."

"Yes?" Devon repeated.

I grinned, but then I forced it back and tried to look unaffected. "No one else would want to go with us, so we might as well go together."

Devon laughed. "True," he said, pretending to frown. "Wouldn't want one of the other guys to have to put up with you. You know that's the real reason I asked you."

I shoved him. "Keep telling yourself that and you'll be lucky if I don't show up dressed like a lobster."

Devon shook his head. "I happen to like lobsters. A lot."

I couldn't help the smile that spread across my face.

Yeah. Maybe I did too.

In a sea of butterflies, I'd found a fellow crustacean.

CHAPTER TWENTY- FOUR

$\mathcal{F}$riday evening my house was in a tizzy. Between the two of us, Dad and I were nervous enough for at least a dozen people. I'd never had a date before. Would Devon and I hold hands? I wasn't sure I even knew how to dance. What if I stepped on his toes?

From the way my father was acting, you'd think he'd never had a real date either. He stood in his bedroom staring at his wardrobe while making horrible, pained faces. Every shirt he owned was either a gray T-shirt or a brick flannel, and all of them had stains or holes. Some had stains *and* holes.

Kitty had directed all the girls to wear black dresses with orange monarch wings, so I'd put on the black dress my mother had bought me during our expedition to the mall, and Ana was on her way over with the butterfly wings she'd made, but I felt sick to my stomach with nerves and I could tell Dad felt the same. He held up an armload of old shirts and grimaced.

"Choose one of the flannels," I advised. I grabbed a dark blue one from the top of the pile. "Here. This one has the smallest tear."

Dad took the shirt and slipped it on, buttoning it up so fast he missed a buttonhole. Then he looked in the mirror, noticed his mistake, and sat down on the bed.

"I can't do this," Dad said, closing his eyes. He gulped, as if he were about to hyperventilate.

"Of course you can," I argued. "It's just a date. I'm the one who should be nervous. At least you've done this before."

"Centuries ago," Dad said. "Jane, look at me. I'm a mess. My hair sticks up. I'm old. Why would anyone want to go out with me? And what the heck am I going to talk about tonight? I'll end up spouting scientific stuff, because you know what? That's all I know about!" He rubbed one hand over his eyes. "I only said yes to make you happy, but now I'm going to call and cancel because there's no way I can go on a date."

I was about to respond, but that's when Ana stepped through the doorway.

In my entire life, I'd never seen Ana look so beautiful.

Her dress scooped down low in the back and she'd pulled her hair up in a French twist. Strands of blond hair framed her face. She wore makeup that highlighted her cheeks, lips, and eyes, and heels that made her seem both taller and older.

My father's mouth fell open. I thought he might say something, but Ana didn't give him a chance. She held out my wings and a black button-down shirt for my dad. Then she put one hand on her hip and gave my father the sharpest look I'd ever seen.

"Emmett James Brannen," she said, "stop your whining."

Dad looked stunned. "Ana?"

"Stand up," Ana said, snapping her fingers. "Take off that old shirt."

Dad did as he was told.

"I bought this new one for you," Ana told him.

"When did you—"

"Shush." She scowled at my shame-faced father. "When are you going to get it through your thick head that you are an attractive, intelligent man?" Ana growled. "You are *not* old, and you are *not* a mess. Now, I get that Susan convinced you that the divorce was all your fault, but that was ten years ago, Emmett. Ten years! And she was one woman. So you are, by god, going to pull yourself together and go on a date."

Ana's whole body trembled. Dad reached out to take

the shirt and their hands met, but neither one pulled away. Finally, she let go. He slipped on the shirt and Ana started to button it up.

"I can do that," Dad said, his voice soft, but Ana shook her head.

"No. You can't. Do you want to know why? Because you're blind, Emmett Brannen. Blind! You can't see a thing even when it's right in front of your face."

Ana fastened the final button and then she whipped around, stomping out of Dad's bedroom and down the stairs.

Dad and I stared after her.

"What do you think's gotten into her?" Dad asked. He'd shaved earlier, and now he patted on some aftershave, running his hand over his jaw.

I sat down on Dad's bed. I thought about the look on Ana's face and the hundreds of times she'd looked at my father as if he were the most incredible person on the planet. Maybe Dad was blind, but I wasn't.

Not anymore.

"Dad," I said, clearing my throat. "I need to tell you something."

"Yeah?"

"That note from Elle Fairfax?"

"Yes."

"Devon wrote it. He wrote a similar one for his mom. From you."

Dad had just picked up his hairbrush, but now he dropped it. "What?"

"Don't be angry," I pleaded. "He was trying to help me. Mom had just said she was filing for custody, and we figured you wouldn't have a chance unless you had someone else on your side, the way Mom has Erik."

"So you kids thought setting me up with Elle Fairfax on *one* date would convince some judge I'm the better parent?" Dad's eyes bulged. "You didn't think Elle and I would discover that neither one of us asked the other out? Jane, what were you thinking?!"

Tears pricked my eyes. "I'm really sorry. I was just . . . scared. So I lied. And I was stupid too, because this whole time you already have someone who loves you. And she's perfect."

Dad's face softened. "You *are* perfect, Jane. Despite your meddling."

I shook my head. "I don't mean me, Dad. I'm talking about Ana."

I expected my father to argue. I waited for him to deny that Ana could possibly have feelings for him, or maybe he'd say I'd misunderstood what I'd seen, but instead he stared at his own reflection in the mirror.

"She does, doesn't she?" he said at last, the words filled with disbelief.

"Yeah," I said. "She does."

"But how can that be?" Dad murmured. "Ana is young and beautiful. She's smart and creative. Brave. Kind. And on top of all that, she's tougher than me. You know that, don't you? Why on earth would she fall in love with someone as plain and awkward as your geeky father?"

I was about to answer, but I didn't have to because Ana stepped back into the room.

"Not only are you blind," she said, "but you also haven't figured out that the walls in this old house are paper thin." She wiped her eyes, smudging her makeup. "You're such a fool, Emmett. I've loved you for years because you are perfect. Perfect for me. I happen to love your scientific babble. And your awkwardness. I think you're the handsomest man I know, and it doesn't matter to me how old you are. You're brilliant and you're an amazing father, and when I'm with you and Jane, my life is complete." She sniffled. "Now do you believe I love you?"

My father laughed, a single surprised guffaw, and his eyes were suspiciously wet.

"Maybe," he said, "but I'll probably need some reminders."

"Fine." Ana stepped up so she and Dad were toe to toe. And then she kissed him.

I wasn't sure whether to laugh or cry. All I knew was that it was time for me to leave them on their own.

CHAPTER TWENTY-FIVE

When we got to the Penmore Estate and drove up the long, winding driveway, I couldn't help thinking about how many times Kitty and I had daydreamed about this place. Now, though, I found I didn't need princesses, knights, or even a magical ball to make this night special. With Dad and Ana holding hands in the cab of the truck, my life was perfect just the way it was.

Outside, the Fairfaxes had draped orange lights around everything, making the entire property sparkle. It was a gorgeous night—clear and cold, with a salty nip in the air. I remembered how I'd been embarrassed because Whickett Harbor smelled like seaweed, but tonight I didn't smell seaweed. I smelled the ocean, vast and powerful, just beyond my sight, giving us clean air to breathe, food to eat, and a home to hundreds of thousands of different species.

I closed my eyes and inhaled.

When I opened my eyes again, Dad and Ana had gotten

out and were waiting for me. All around us, people were exiting their vehicles and I could tell that the chaperones were going to outnumber the kids. Half the adults in Whickett Harbor had invited themselves.

"I suppose I ought to head in first to make my apologies to Elle," Dad said, letting go of Ana's hand.

The whole way over, I'd been worrying about Elle's reaction. After all she'd done for me, she didn't deserve to be disappointed, but there was no way around it.

"Let me do that, okay Dad?" I said. "Devon's the one who wrote the note, but I knew it was fake and I let you guys believe it. I'll apologize. Then you can talk to her afterward."

Dad glanced at Ana, but then they both nodded.

"We'll take a walk around the grounds. You've got fifteen minutes," Dad said.

"Got it." I ran ahead, dodging between crowds of people and ducking under low branches. It was hard to run in a dress and flats, but I managed. When I reached the front door, Devon stood there scanning the crowd. When he saw me, he grinned.

"You've got leaves in your hair," he said. "And there's mud splattered on your legs."

I ran my hand over my hair and plucked out a few stray leaves. "Drat."

Devon shook his head. "It's okay. You look just right."

He was wearing a tuxedo. Yes, a tuxedo. It figured that a woman who would send her children to school in sweater vests and ties would make them wear tuxedos to the school dance. Devon caught me studying him and flushed.

"Mom made me and Matthew wear these. I know. It's overkill."

I laughed. "Well, you're certainly the best-dressed guys in Whickett Harbor. Maybe even the whole state of Maine."

Devon sighed. He held out his elbow the way men did in the movies. "Shall we go in?"

I linked my arm with his. "Yes. Only we have to talk to your mother right away. My father knows that the note was a fake, and I promised I'd apologize. He's coming to the dance with Ana." My face heated a thousand degrees. "Do you think your mom will be mad?"

Devon winced. "I don't know."

I hated the thought of Elle being angry. I was about to say something, but then we stepped inside and I gasped. The foyer was decorated with hundreds of tiny orange lights and glittering streamers. The banister of the spiral staircase had been draped with orange beaded garland, and the chandelier overhead sparkled. All around the perimeter of the room were milkweed plants in decorative pots.

"Wow! This place looks amazing."

Devon let go of my arm. "Jane," he said, "there's something you should know."

I was instantly suspicious. "What is it?"

"Your mother did the decorating. She and Erik insisted. They arrived this morning, and they've been working all day. They brought in the milkweed from a greenhouse in New Hampton, and after the dance they're donating them to the school so we can create a monarch garden. Erik has been setting up the cameras and lighting, and your mum—" He paused. "I gave her your article to read."

I swallowed hard. "You did?"

Devon nodded. "Please don't be angry. She cried when she read it. I think she must have read it about ten times by now, and then Erik read it." He studied me. "Are you upset?"

I shook my head. "No. I think part of me was writing it to her all along. I mean, I thought about the rest of the people who'd read it too, but mostly I wanted my mom to see Dad and Whickett Harbor through my eyes for once."

"Well, I hope it worked," Devon said. He tilted his head toward the spiral staircase where my mother was standing. She looked gorgeous. Her dark hair was done up in an elegant braided style and she wore a black mermaid dress that swept the floor at her feet. A diamond choker accented her long neck, and tiny diamond earrings were in her ears. If I wasn't mistaken, they were the same ones she'd worn in our mother-daughter photo.

Mom saw me and hesitated. She gulped in a huge breath before she made her way down the stairs. I knew I needed to find Elle before Dad and Ana came in, but right now, I couldn't walk away from my mother.

"Hi," she said when she reached me.

"Hi."

"Jane, I've been—"

"Mom, I need to—"

We started talking at the same time, and then we both stopped. "You first," Mom said. "It's been suggested that I ought to listen to my daughter more often, so I may as well start now."

My eyes widened in surprise. Who had suggested that? Dad? Erik?

I took a deep breath. "Mom, I don't want to live with you and Erik. Not now, and not ever. Not even part-time. I'm sure that California is an amazing place, and I think that Erik is a great guy, but Whickett Harbor is my home and I love it here. I know that when you were my age, you were miserable in Maine, but I'm not like you. Dad and Ana and I . . . we're happy. And I know that you think I won't be able to find things to write about if I'm not on a movie set, but I will. I already have. You and Erik can fight for custody, but why would you want to take someone away from the place where they're happiest?"

To my surprise, my mother didn't interrupt. She listened and nodded, and when I was through, she said, "You're right."

I waited for more. Where were the theatrical tears? The begging and pleading? Why was she so . . . calm?

"I'm right?" I said, wondering if I'd heard her correctly.

"Yes," Mom said. "I owe you an apology, Jane. Many of them, actually. I know you think that the only reason I came here to Whickett Harbor was to convince you to move to California with me and Erik. And . . . you're right. That is why I came. I told myself you'd want to leave, that I'd be doing you a favor, and this was the only way I could hold on to Erik. But I've been informed that I was wrong. He loves me no matter what."

She glanced over, and I turned to see Erik and Matthew rigging up some sort of cart with a camera on it. Erik had on black pants and a sport coat, but even on a cold October night he still wore flip-flops.

Erik waved when he saw us looking over, and Mom and I waved back.

"I'm sorry I used you, Jane. And I'm sorry I'm not a better mother. I wish I knew how."

"How to be a mom?"

Mom nodded. "I just . . . don't know the right things to do. I've never known how to be your mother."

"Well, you could ask me, you know."

Mom laughed. "Could I? What would you say I could do to be a better mom?"

"For starters, you could call me more often. And when we talk on the phone you can tell me real stuff about your life—like that you got engaged, for example—and you could ask about real stuff in my life. Learn the names of my friends. Visit once in a while. Instead of pretending everything is already perfect between us, we could get to know each other for real."

"I'd like that," Mom said. Her eyes were watery, but she didn't burst into tears, although I could tell she wanted to.

"We could talk about writing more too," I added. "I have all kinds of questions about screenwriting, but you're always too busy telling me about the movie stars and directors and what parties you went to that we never get to talk about the part I'd actually find interesting. I don't care about the flashy stuff. I want to know about what you do."

This time, I could tell Mom hadn't seen that coming. Her eyes opened wide. "But I thought you'd be bored by my job. I don't do anything exciting."

"It's exciting to me."

"Okay then," Mom said. "Writing is definitely something I can talk about." She paused. "Speaking of which . . . your article was really well written, Jane. I've always bragged about you being a great writer because I thought that's what a mother ought to do, but from now on I'll say it because I mean it. You really are the next great Jane."

"Even though you never liked Jane Austen?"

Mom laughed. "Well, there are lots of great Janes in history. You don't have to follow in anyone else's footsteps. I have a feeling you'll create your own path."

"Thanks."

We stood there for a moment, neither one of us sure what to say next.

"Jane," Mom said, "if Erik and I withdraw the custody filing, would you consider coming to visit us more often? Not because a court makes you do it but because we'd like to spend time with you? Maybe two weeks at Christmas and two weeks in the summer to start?"

I hesitated. I was so used to thinking of my mother as the villain that it was hard to change my mind, but finally I nodded. "Sure."

"And," my mother added, "when it's time for Erik and me to get married, would you be my maid of honor?"

My cheeks heated with a mix of pleasure and embarrassment. I looked down at my mud-spattered legs and thought about the kind of glamorous wedding my mother and Erik would plan. I'd probably arrive with scraped knees and spill stuff on my dress.

"Are you sure?"

"One hundred percent."

"Then okay. I'll try my best."

Mom smiled, and then she reached out to hug me. I couldn't remember the last time my mother had hugged me for real. Not some quick, fake hug, but an honest-to-goodness embrace where she held me tight and buried her face in my hair.

"I love you, Jane," Mom whispered, and she was crying now, but I didn't mind.

"I love you too."

Maybe we weren't the model mother and daughter, but we were all right. Then a strong pair of arms circled us both. Erik.

"Group hug?" he said, and before we had time to answer, he'd pulled in Kitty and Matthew and everyone else who was standing nearby. "Come on, people. Get in on the love."

We laughed and hugged until Erik yelled, "Cut," and then everyone dispersed. Kitty grabbed my elbow as soon as Mom and Erik walked away.

"So? Is she dropping the custody filing?"

A huge grin spread across my face. "Yes."

Kitty nearly burst into tears. "And are you really here as Devon's date? He told Matthew you were, but I said I wouldn't believe it unless I heard it from you."

I blushed from the tips of my ears to the tips of my toes. "Actually, I am."

"But I thought you hated Devon Fairfax."

"I've been told on good authority that hate is often the start of love."

Kitty scrunched up her nose. "What does that even mean, Jane?"

"It means that sometimes feelings change." I paused. "Sorry I didn't tell you right away. I didn't know how to say it, and I thought you might feel like I was trying to steal the spotlight from you and Matthew. You guys are really great together, but me and Devon . . ."

". . . are just as great in your own unique way," Kitty said. She laughed, squeezing my hand. "Don't you realize what this means?"

I shook my head.

"It means that our childhood dreams could come true. We really could have a double wedding right here at the Penmore Estate!"

"Kitty," I said, "don't you think that it's a little too soon to start planning our weddings?"

"Pish posh," Kitty said in her best Welsh accent. "Don't

you dare squash my—" Then she stopped mid-sentence. "Are your dad and Ana holding hands?"

I looked over to where she was staring, and saw that my father and Ana had just walked through the front door, hand in hand.

"Oh no," I said. "I need to find Elle. Immediately."

"Isn't your father supposed to be here with—"

"Yes!" I said. "Where is she?"

I felt sick thinking of Elle being stood up by my dad. Kitty shook her head and we both scanned the room.

"Maybe she's upstairs?" Kitty suggested.

I had to find Elle before she saw Dad and Ana. I dashed up the steps, ignoring the people who tried to say hello. There was a third floor where the bedrooms were located, but before I went up there, I thought I'd try her office, just in case.

I opened the door, and there sat Elle Fairfax, leaning back in her chair behind her mahogany desk. I was out of breath from my sprint, so I gulped in air. Elle raised an eyebrow at my breathless state.

"You're late," she chided.

"Late?" I managed to huff out.

"I was getting worried."

I had no idea what she was talking about, but I didn't have time for riddles today.

"I have something to tell you," I blurted. "That note,

asking you to the dance, it wasn't from my father. Devon wrote it, but he did it for me because I thought my dad needed a partner. Someone who could upstage Erik so a judge wouldn't grant my mother custody. I thought that since you're a famous author with lots of money, you could help us. I'm so, so sorry. I used you, just like my mom was using me, and . . . I didn't mean to hurt you. Especially after you helped me."

As the story came pouring out I kept waiting for the moment when Elle's face would turn into an angry or shocked expression. Any minute now, she'd tell me what a thoughtless, selfish human being I was, and how I was completely unworthy of dating her son.

Instead, her face softened.

"Jane, Jane, Jane," she tsked. "Do you think I actually believed that your father wrote his notes on Hello Kitty notecards?"

I sucked in a breath. "You noticed that?"

"Of course," Elle said. "It's an author's job to notice the details." She paused. "But even if I *had* missed that, do you honestly think I wouldn't recognize my own son's handwriting?"

"Oh." That had never occurred to me. "But if you knew my dad didn't write the note, why didn't you tell him the truth?"

"Because," Elle said, "sometimes good love stories need a nudge." She paused. "Your father is here with Ana tonight, isn't he?"

"How did you know?" I said, unable to keep the shock out of my voice.

Elle laughed. "Well, I genuinely like your dad, but anyone with eyes could see the way those two look at each other. I figured it out on the boat trip, but it was clear that they'd been stuck in their rut for quite some time and might never get out of it on their own. So, I added a plot twist. A sprinkle of jealousy. A dash of desire." She shrugged. "Works every time."

My eyes popped.

"So you knew the invitation was fake, but you played along because you wanted Ana to be jealous? You were—"

"Pulling their strings?" Elle laughed. "Why of course, Jane. That's what an author does, isn't it?" She stood and walked around her desk. "Now, I believe we are needed downstairs if there is to be a happy ending to this festive occasion. And there must be a happy ending, at least in *my* books." She winked. "Are you ready to join the others?"

I couldn't help the laughter that burst out, filling the room. This entire night felt surreal, as if I were a character in one of J. E. Fairfax's novels. For a brief moment, I thought how funny it would be if my entire town were made up, all of us characters in someone else's story. Then I shook myself. Real life beckoned.

"Let's go," I said.

Elle and I linked arms, just as I'd done with Devon on the way in. We left the office and walked down the hallway and then we stopped at the top of the spiral stairs, looking below. Kitty had put on a slow song, and Dad and Ana were dancing in the center of the floor, oblivious to everyone around them. Mom and Erik were helping Matthew and Kitty. Miss Bates stood off to one side, swaying to the rhythm. Granny V was helping the girls from my class get their monarch wings on.

And Devon stood at the bottom of the stairs, looking up, waiting for me.

"What do you think?" Elle asked. "Is everything the way you wished it would be?"

I nodded. "Everything is perfect."

Elle smiled and gave me a gentle push. "Then go on," she said. "Enjoy your happily ever after."

AUTHOR'S NOTE

*E*very author has *their* favorite authors, and Jane Austen is one of mine. Like so many fans of her work, I've loved her endearing characters, her fun plot twists, and her happily-ever-afters.

Jane Austen was an English writer who lived from 1775 to 1817. She was one of eight children, and she first began writing as a child. She went on to publish six major novels, all of which have been reprinted many times, translated worldwide, adapted into countless movies and plays, and reimagined in all kinds of ways. She's one of the best-known authors of all time!

My intent with *The Next Great Jane* was not to modernize any specific work of Austen's, but rather to celebrate Jane Austen's writing by incorporating some of my favorite elements from multiple books and infusing the story with the same spirit that I enjoy in her work.

Jane Austen wrote at a time in history when female writers were neither encouraged nor celebrated. She never did get to put her name on her novels during her lifetime, but it's thanks to writers like her that writers like me can practice our craft.

The lab where Jane's father works was based on the Bigelow Laboratory in Maine. It's a privately funded, nonprofit institution that is a global leader in the study of marine ecosystems.

Bigelow labs provides unbiased data, helps shape environmental policy, provides mentorship to the upcoming generation of scientists, creates and invests in new technology, and works to monitor and protect the world's oceans. Their research gives me hope that we *will* combat climate change, protect species diversity, and hand over a beautiful world to the next generation.

A portion of the proceeds from *The Next Great Jane* will be donated to Bigelow Laboratory for Ocean Sciences (www.bigelow.org) in East Boothbay, Maine.

ACKNOWLEDGMENTS

I owe a special thank-you to one of Bigelow laboratory's senior scientists, Nick Record, PhD, who carved out time to meet with me, shared stories about his career, patiently explained the science behind his research, and helped me to bring Jane's father and his work to life. Thanks to Nick and to all of the scientists at Bigelow!

My family not only has roots in Maine going back many generations, but we also have a history of finding true love in Maine. My parents were high school sweethearts who are coming up on fifty years of marriage, and my grandparents Lindsay Going and Alice Brannen were fifth-grade sweethearts in Kennebunkport, Maine. They've been together ever since and are about to celebrate their seventieth wedding anniversary!

I'd like to give a shout-out to all of my Maine extended family. To the Goings and the Brannens, the Bedards and the Adamses, the Devitts, Jackmans, Davises, and Cotes . . . love to you all!

Thank you to my parents, William and Linda Going, to my husband, Dustin Adams, and, my son, Ashton Adams, for their unwavering love and support. Without them, this book would never have gotten finished.

My sincere gratitude goes out to Jack and Nisha Comstock, my co-teachers at the Homestead School in Glen Spey, New York. When I thought I couldn't get this novel done on time, they said, "How can we support you?" Without their progressive attitude, I wouldn't be able to manage both writing and teaching. I also owe a debt of gratitude to my students. Seeing their dedication to protecting our planet makes me want to share their passion with everyone.

Thanks to Clara Gillow Clark, who was an early champion of this novel and who read and critiqued many different drafts. The Highlights Foundation also provided sacred space to focus on my writing at two critical junctures. Invaluable.

Finally, to my agent, Ginger Knowlton, and my editor, Kathy Dawson . . . thank you so much for your patience, your encouragement, and for all the work you do on my behalf. I'm tremendously grateful.